THI

Over the years I've worked in a variety of different areas; most were unsatisfying. School served me well, if the dovetail joint and north Atlantic drift might be considered useful information, those being the only things I learnt there. Needless to say, I didn't really pay much attention.

In business for thirteen years, waste management, I've also turned my hand to air filter manufacture, haulage and web-design. This is my first novel.

Future titles to be released
by Graham James

- *The Running Day*
- *Construction*

www.gjstories.net

GRAHAM JAMES

The Horizon Trap

<u>HADO</u>

Hado Publications
Advantage Business Centre
132-134 Great Ancoats Street
Manchester - M4 6DE

A Paperback Original 2014
1

ISBN: 978-0-9928780-0-9

Printed and bound in Great Britain by
Talbot Print Services

The paper used in this publication
is from a sustainable source.

ACKNOWLEDGMENTS

Quantum physics, with its non-local quality, is perhaps the most puzzling enquiry science can address. This fascinating subject, stranger than fiction, provides the backdrop to this novel.

It is with grateful thanks to the editing skill and research of Jessica Augustsson and Johannes Svensson that this book finds its place. A special thanks must go to family, Aunt Margaret, whose kind assistance proved invaluable, and everyone else who helped ensure the book's final completion. Thanks also to John Talbot for providing printing and good advice. Finally, thanks must go to the scientists and visionaries out there without whom complex scientific knowledge might otherwise go unobserved. In their discoveries, and willingness to share, lay the seeds of every science fiction author's beginning.

Please note, some of the spellings and phrases in this book are used to reflect its setting in America.

PROLOGUE

Southeast Asia, 1974

Major Baxley wiped the sweat off his forehead as he watched the archaeologists and Burmese soldiers clear out the rubble from the collapse. The government official who had been assigned to monitor the activities of the expedition looked on disapprovingly from the sidelines. It was just lucky that it was one of their soldiers and not one of Baxley's archaeologists who had triggered the collapse or the whole expedition might have been cut short right then and there.

Still, not even the cold stare of bureaucracy could detract from the excitement of the moment. Coming here had been a matter of nostalgia really, returning to a land with which he had long been fascinated. He recalled the first time a local guide had shown him the temples while he was stationed here during the war. Back then this area had been in the process of being mapped, an unknown country, wild and inhospitable. The men under his command—worn down by the oppressive heat and humidity—had hated the jungle and everything about it, but Baxley had always felt an affinity for it that he had been at a loss to clearly explain, even to himself. He had found the beauty of the country and the majesty of the ancient buildings breathtaking, the way the spires and domes of the ancient temples broke the treetop vista here and there as if they were keeping watch over the jungle landscape.

It had taken him some time to get around to coming back here, more than twenty years in fact. He had often considered returning, but it had seemed frivolous to travel just to see the place. That was the way tourists explored the world and he didn't want to return as a tourist. Finally, his retirement, and money raised from friends and family, afforded the opportunity to organise something more worthwhile.

An archaeological expedition was something a man could be proud to be part of, something that would be a benefit to all mankind, or at least the part that went to museums.

Secretly he had been prepared for disappointment, afraid that his memories had been twisted by the passage of time into some ideal fantasy that reality would never be able to measure up to, afraid that there was nothing of significance left to find, that his expedition would be a wild goose chase through a hostile jungle, but he had found that despite the passage of time and the difference of circumstances, the country had lost none of its appeal to him.

And now the carelessness of a soldier had exposed a hitherto unknown entrance into one of the temple buildings, transforming the selfish fancy of an aging man into a successful enterprise in its own right. As soon as enough of the rubble had been cleared, the Major was the first one through the door despite the danger of further collapse. Inside there was a steeply ascending spiral staircase whose narrow steps he followed up to a small chamber sealed off from the rest of the structure.

What purpose the room could have served when the structure was built he did not know, but it seemed to be some sort of shrine, as the one central feature was a plain stone altar bearing a single dusty wooden chest. Major Baxley, irresistibly drawn to the object, crept forward on his hands and knees to avoid banging his head against the low ceiling.

Up close he could see that there were carved symbols along the edges of the wood, and also inlaid tablets with further symbols all along the sides of the box. Carefully, Major Baxley leaned forward and tried to blow away the dust, creating an impressive cloud but not revealing much of the imagery beneath it. Frustrated he set down his electric torch and started to wipe off the remaining dust with his still damp handkerchief.

The designs he unveiled would follow him in his dreams for the rest of his life. They were unlike any symbols he had seen anywhere else and they seemed to dance around the edges of the chest and the faces of the inlaid tablets to unheard music.

When the stone-faced government official confiscated the chest the next day as a cultural treasure of Burma, Major Baxley wept openly, convinced in his heart that the most important thing he had ever laid eyes on was now slipping out of his grasp forever.

ONE

I

Present day, Washington D.C.

Kim Knowles leaned back from the monitor in front of her, wondering for the seventh time that evening what the hell she was doing. The specs for the changes were straightforward enough but the ultimate purpose was a bit of a mystery. She had joined Sytek because it seemed to be a chance to do some interesting research in a creative environment *not* run by some multinational corporation only interested in making money. Sytek was founded by Darius Daucourt, along with a Russian colleague of his, Igor Bobrik, to independently pursue research that interested them both. It had seemed to

Kim at the time that this showed strength of character and integrity and when she was approached about joining the company she jumped at the chance.

Now they were remodelling all their systems to be able to interface with unknown technology being sent to them by one of the largest and most influential companies of the world. Bionamic had started as a British pharmaceutical company but had rapidly expanded into other areas. Currently, their main interest was in communications technology with sidelines into almost anything connected to technology or medicine. The Managing Director of Bionamic was a man named Max Kohler. Kim had only seen him on TV but though he was all smiles and pretty words for the cameras, she had found his manner abrasive somehow.

Regardless of the virtues of Max Kohler, Bionamic was definitely not associated with integrity in Kim's mind. In fact, when she had still been a student she had once signed an online petition against them. She seemed to recall it having to do with the mishandling of medical waste, but she'd been protesting many things when she was young and couldn't remember the details.

She sighed and returned to her work, turning the list of parameters to another page and entering the appropriate adjustments into the system. Over at another machine, Potter had finished installing high capacity fibre connectors to the main servers and was engrossed in reading through the reams of surplus documentation that Bionamic had sent over along with the specs for the changes.

"Find anything interesting?" Kim asked while entering the final adjustments to some of their analytical software.

"Huh?" Potter looked up at her as if he'd forgotten she was there. The others—spread out throughout the cluttered room, engaged in tasks of their own—looked up from their work, eager for anything that might explain what they were going to be working on.

"Oh," Potter said finally, looking around at the others. "I don't know. Some of these calculations make me think we are finally treading into my territory. Quarks and quanta, here we come." A grin spread across his face making him look ten years younger.

Dave, who was monitoring a systems check running on the backup server, chuckled at this.

"You can tell that just from the math, huh?"

"Sure I can. They don't hand out PhDs to just anyone, you know." Kim watched Dave roll his eyes at this. "Also," Potter continued, "there is a reference here to something called a sub-quantum visual-cerebral interface. Whatever the hell that is."

"So much for the math detective," Dave snickered.

Any reply from Potter was cut short as Darius and Igor walked into the lab. They stopped by the railing of the raised walkway surrounding "the drum," a term everyone used to describe that part of the room given over to experiments, and Darius smiled down at them all.

"How are you coming along?" Darius asked.

"Almost done," Kim said, and the others echoed her sentiments.

"Good. I want to apologise for not being as straightforward with you about this as I have been about projects in the past. I want you to know that this has entirely been at the request of Bionamic, who want to protect their intellectual property to the fullest. The good news is that the non-disclosure agreements you signed have been duly processed and I am now allowed to let you in on the secrets."

With a nod at Igor, Darius walked over to the large wall-mounted screen at one end of the lab while Igor took his position at the computer that controlled it. A map of the world promptly appeared.

Darius looked up at the screen and then to the assembled team, nodding to Igor again.

"Here is England, and here we are," Igor began, symbols on the screen indicating the things he talked about. "The distance between these two points, some three thousand seven hundred miles is about to be reduced to zero."

"Not actually, of course," Darius grinned. "Some of you," he said, and Kim felt his eyes lingering on hers for a second, "have asked why I have even considered working with a big company like Bionamic when Sytek was created to be an independent operator. A free agent, so to speak. The answer is that they have twisted my arm. With science."

There was a pause and Kim sat up straighter in her chair as Darius continued. "We have been invited to join forces with them in a cross-Atlantic experiment in information transfer through particle entanglement."

Kim frowned. "Entanglement?" She looked

over at Potter but he seemed to be as surprised as she was. "I was under the impression that this sort of thing was still largely theoretical. I didn't realise anybody was covering these sort of distances."

"Nobody is," Potter said. "Not that I am aware of, anyway."

"Apparently, Bionamic have been testing these systems for years, certainly long enough before they contacted us, but Mr. Potter is right. Nobody is covering these distances. Yet. Hopefully we will be the first."

Igor tapped at the keyboard in front of him and the picture on the screen changed. "This is the device that initiates the entanglement. It's a fractal charged phase conjugating photonic duplicator, which they've imaginatively entitled the Dupo. It's only half the story though."

Igor changed the screen's image once more. "There! This is their masterpiece. This is where all the interesting stuff happens."

Bionamic's second device, which was one of a pair, was about two feet in circumference and stood about three feet tall. It was painted in industry blue and looked something similar to a large fanned electro-magnetic motor.

"A magnetic octopole radio-frequency trap. One of these things can store over ten to the 9th entangled particles," he emphasised, "but it manages to sustain and protect the entanglement indefinitely, at least as far as we can make out. It's called an IPAS, which stands for inverse particle advanced storage."

"So, basically the Dupo ejects the entangled particles, an IPAS collects them, then it's onto a ship, or whatever, for one unit, which is then transported to any location across the planet. Is that about it?" Dave asked.

"Basically," Igor replied. "It is possible to use fibre-optics to transport the entangled particles between devices, but only for shorter distances or they lose their entangled state." Kim looked at the big screen trying to find some flaw that would make the project less appealing, but she couldn't think of one. Objectively, it was the opportunity of a lifetime. Still, something didn't feel quite right about the whole thing regardless of her opinions of Bionamic.

Before Kim could put a voice to her misgivings, Ray broke in with a question. Ray was one of the elders, a renowned physicist in his own right. "You say that Bionamic's been working on this for several years?"

"That's right," Darius replied. "From what I've gathered in talking to Max, their trial runs over in the UK have ironed out almost every fault. In fact, we should be good to go as soon as our IPAS arrives in the lab. That should be sometime in the next few weeks."

"So what do they need us for?" Ray asked. "I'm sorry. I know we're all competent experts in our fields, with the possible exception of Dave." He grinned over at the younger man who was muttering something barely audible about senile old men. "But Bionamic has more resources than Santa Claus. They certainly have offices and labs in the states. Why don't they operate both sides of the link themselves?"

"From what Max told me, they already have their best people working on their side, and they are reluctant to split the team. Besides, they want fresh input and since they are not about to publish a paper on their theories before they have finalised their designs..." He let the words hang and gestured to Igor who went into a more detailed technical overview.

Kim found much of it hard to follow—not the technical details, but a degree in scientific engineering didn't cover much of the specifics of quantum theory. She knew of entanglement,

18

of course, where two particles or atoms were brought into alignment and somehow a bond was forged between them so that if you changed the state of one of the particles, a corresponding change would instantaneously happen to the other, no matter what the distance was between them. If this experiment worked, it would mean that information could pass from one continent to the other without crossing the intervening distance. Two computers communicating this way would mean instantaneous information exchange and this was what Bionamic was aiming for on a big scale. A quantum internet. Even further into the future, technology like this could allow space probes light years away to transfer their gathered data instantaneously, and the potential uses didn't stop there.

Sytek's initial trials, Kim gathered, would be to route signals between the two labs through the entanglement, but the eventual goal was for all computers to eventually be able to connect into a quantum internet, eliminating latency and the need for cables altogether.

After the presentation, Darius and Igor joined the others in the drum and got involved in the remaining preparations. Igor joined

Melanie and Tony, both of whom had been handpicked by Darius as soon as they'd finished their PhDs, and started to go through some of the science behind the connection in detail. Ray, intrigued by anything he hadn't completely mastered, wandered over to join them. Darius on the other hand walked straight over to Kim and sat down in the seat next to her.

"I'm sorry I couldn't tell you before," he said. "I know you still have misgivings, but I couldn't pass this up. No matter who holds the reins it is going to be a fantastic project. Apart from the financial remuneration, and that is substantial, it will make us a name. It will open doors for this company that I could never have dreamed of touching without something like this under our belt."

Kim sat silent for a moment, searching his eyes for something other than sincerity. Finally she sighed and sank back in her chair. "Just promise me we will pull out if it turns out we're being used to help take over the world, okay?" Darius laughed and Kim couldn't help but smile. He had a nice laugh.

"I promise," he said.

As he stood up, she caught his hand to

prevent him from leaving. "What's he like?"

"Who?"

"Max Kohler, mighty head of Bionamic," she replied.

She let his hand go and he stroked his chin. "You know, I'm not sure," he said. "In some ways he's the most annoying man I've talked to, but somehow you just can't bring yourself to hate the man. No matter how much you'd like to." He shrugged and quirked up one side of his mouth in a half-smile. At that moment, Potter looked up from the papers he was going through and called Darius over. Together they bent over the documents and fell into deep conversation. Kim watched them for a while before returning to her screen and the blinking cursor that was trying to get her attention.

II

New York City, Four nights later

Scott Guest was in the locker room at National Electronics trying to let go of the strain of another nightshift. He hurled his rolled-up gloves onto the top of the locker and kicked off his boots, then sat down heavily on the bench seat and rested his head in his hands.

The locker room hadn't seen a makeover in years, aside from the occasional sweep when the janitor managed to find the place. As it was, the room felt more like a no-go zone than a locker room, its windows painted the same colour as the walls.

"So, Scott, you still coming or what?" The voice belonged to Joe Sands. They weren't exactly close friends but they watched the occasional ballgame together and invited each other to barbeques and parties.

"Yeah, I already told you I would. When is it again?"

"Couple of weeks. Tina's gonna drive us all down there. We're staying at my sister's house, remember, so you won't even have to pay for a hotel."

"Won't that put a damper on the wedding night?" Scott raised an eyebrow.

"Nah, they fly out for their honeymoon the same day. I'm watching the house for them, so it'll be party time for all *vatos locos* !" Joe joked with a grin. Seeing another friend wander past the open door he called out after him and said a hurried goodbye to Scott before disappearing out the door.

Scott wasn't really looking forward to Joe's Washington trip and would rather have stayed in New York with his friends. The fact that Joe's sister was tying the knot meant nothing to him; he neither knew her nor cared to, and though he enjoyed the occasional party, he had the feeling that a whole week in the company of Joe and his drinking buddies might be a bit much.

The people Scott normally hung out with weren't the types to go out and get drunk just for kicks and the typical conversation would revolve more about who had been hacking who, or the latest scientific development, rather than what team won the super bowl and which supermodel they'd like to sleep with. He had learned from experience that Joe's friends and his didn't really mix well, so there was no point in asking if he could bring any of them.

He had been determined to find some way to back out of the trip altogether when the rumour had reached him that an old friend of his had been hired by Sytek, and that Sytek had been picked up by Bionamic for some sort of unannounced project. Finding hard inside information on Bionamic was next to impossible; if he could somehow arrange to talk to Kim in Washington perhaps he could get something useful from her. Maybe she could even be convinced to help. They had been able to rustle up Kim's Washington address, but Scott really had no idea if she would want to talk to him or not, much less if she would want to help, but he had to try. Sue would never forgive him if he didn't.

TWO

I

Once the final word was given and the final signature was in place, Darius was amazed at the speed with which Bionamic set the operation into motion. They'd employed the services of a local cable television company to oversee the network installation and any subsequent connections to the public, all of which was well under way within a month.

The public had been introduced to the enterprise through a televised lottery where five hundred lucky patrons were selected to test "the internet of the future". The five hundred Americans who would have connections to Sytek would be directly linked via the entangled connection to Bionamic on the other side, before being routed to the normal internet from there. Correspondingly, there were five hundred households in the UK who were being bounced over to Sytek and then connected to the normal internet on this side of the Atlantic.

Strictly speaking of course, it wasn't a true quantum internet, but this hadn't prevented Bionamic's PR team from advertising their vision of what life would be like with one.

Normally, just getting the permits for laying down the fibre would have taken months, but Max had stated that his people would deal with the legal side, and true to his word they had delivered all the relevant legal documents less than two weeks later. Darius was happy to leave that kind of thing to someone else. He found staying in the lab to watch the arrival and integration of Sytek's IPAS devices to be a much more rewarding prospect.

It was during one of their videoconferences about the project that Darius finally got around to asking Max about the device that had been found referenced among the documentation Bionamic had sent them. First Potter and later Potter and Dave together had been pushing him to find out more about it and so finally, mostly to get them to stop bothering him on the subject, he had brought up the question.

"The feedback interface?" Max furrowed his brow on the screen on Darius's desk. "That wasn't part of the documentation we sent you."

"It was in there. Not the whole thing, but enough references and diagrams to have two of my people up in arms about wanting more details. I've told them it's probably some throw-away project that didn't even work, but they won't take my word for it. Anything you can do to stem the tide would be appreciated."

"Oh, it worked alright. I'm just not sure it's the sort of thing you should be messing around with."

"Then what the hell is it?" Darius demanded. "Sub-quantum visual-cerebral interface sounds like that much nonsense to me."

Max somehow managed to look apologetic and superior at the same time. "Well. In the early days of the tests, one of our engineers was looking into some feedback noise coming from the entanglement. To help him track down what was causing it, he put a visual representation of it up on a screen. His final report was quite fanciful, talking of patterns in the feedback." He shrugged. "Of course I dismissed it and since the feedback didn't seem to have any practical effect on what was going on, the report was filed and forgotten. By me anyway."

Darius said nothing. He was a bit astonished that this device Potter had been obsessing about the last couple of weeks seemed to have some basis in reality after all. Potter was a brilliant physicist but he could sometimes get carried away by his own enthusiasm. Darius had assumed this was one of those cases.

"Some time later one of my scientists happened across the report and was fascinated by it, especially the parts claiming it was possible to interpret the feedback as points in a three-dimensional space. So he tinkered with it in his spare time. The SQ interface is what he came up with. A direct virtual connection to the entanglement-feedback, with brain stimulation action." Max smirked. "With practice you are supposed to actually see the data as an environment around you. I tried it once myself but all I could see was green noise."

"You said something about it being dangerous," Darius interjected, gauging that Max's interest in talking about this was running low.

"Yes I did. Apparently certain areas of the brain get very active while trying to decipher the noise from the feedback, so the device stimulates the activity in those areas to try to help the process. Listening to the guy who came up with them, it sounds like some sort of transcendental meditation or something. I don't know how it works, but I would think twice about letting a machine mess with my brain."

Darius nodded. "I see what you mean. I'll tell my guys to let sleeping dogs lie."

Max shrugged again. "Hey, it's no skin off my nose if they want to poke around in it. I'll even send them what we've got on it, just make sure they know they are doing it on their own time and at their own risk."

The sudden turnabout felt a bit strange and Darius found himself trying to figure out why Max was so forthcoming all of a sudden. He was also a bit worried about what else the man was holding back on. "So other than this brain-conditioning feedback, is there anything else you aren't telling us?"

"Look, it's not something you needed to know," Max explained. "It isn't going to affect the day-to-day usage of the technology. The people participating in our tests certainly won't have the kind of access that gives them a direct line to the resonance feedback, and even then the only way it could come back and bite us is if those plans get out and some idiot fries his brain trying to recreate the feedback interface. All the more reason not to bandy the information about, don't you think? We were going to go back and try to figure it out, at some point, but it's a bit beyond our grasp as it is."

"It's that incomprehensible?"

"Worse!" Max grunted. "It defies all known logic! It might not even be real, might be a brain-ghost of people staring for too long into static. It simply wouldn't have been fair to bring something like that to your attention before the launch. You certainly don't need more to cope with over there."

Leaving his office Darius headed into the lab where Igor was giving a speech. Half-listening to the man's technical jargon filling the room, he stared at their IPAS device, which was securely mounted on a chrome podium near the edge of the lab floor. They'd already started to use the connection and it was fast. The information was literally in two places at once as soon as you pressed send, something he wasn't entirely sure he'd ever get used to.

"It's something else isn't it?" Tony asked as he passed Darius on his way out of the room.

"It is."

"Listen, Darius, I've been meaning to thank you. Properly, I mean. I never imagined myself getting a job this interesting, not in a million years."

"You're welcome, Tony. What's Igor going on about over there?"

"He's going over some of the specifics of the theory."

Darius nodded.

"You know, I was thinking about it all last night," Tony continued. "I couldn't sleep. I kept going over the things we talk about, here at work, and trying to get my head around the fact that these are not just theory lectures. That we are actually going to use it in a practical application. It really is the kind of thing I've always dreamt of getting my hands on."

"I'm glad you're enjoying it." Darius found himself smiling as Tony rejoined the others. In his mind, this was what science was about. Making your dreams come true.

As promised, the papers on the feedback interface arrived the next morning and Darius handed them to Potter with the caution that any work they did on it was outside the project and that they were to take all possible precautions. Potter received the documentation, and the news that Bionamic would be sending one of the prototype interface devices by special courier, with his usual worrying glee. Before the evening was out, he had hooked up a computer and a monitor to the IPAS, filling the screen with green shapes that somewhat resembled the sky; that is if the sky had been filled with green magnetic clouds. When Darius left the lab late that night, he could see Potter sitting by his desk staring into the screen and taking notes.

When the prototype arrived a few days later, it was remarkable—just like everything else created by Bionamic. It had been constructed exclusively from high-end materials: a stable plastic composite interwoven with fibres of germanium and housing as much state-of-the-art electronics as would fit inside the casing. Along the frame were dots of highly conductive metal that supposedly connected to the vital spots of the forehead and temples to read and stimulate the brain. It was slick, size-adjustable and stylish, looking more like a finished product than a research prototype.

Darius noticed that Potter wasted no time "getting to know" the device, as he put it, and in the week leading up to launch, he had to be cautioned several times to not let his obsession get the better of him.

II

For Kim, launch night so far had not been the celebration she had hoped it would be. After the final tests had been performed and the whole system turned on at once for the first time, she had cheered with the rest of them, but somehow during dinner all she could think of was how they were now connected to Bionamic and Max Kohler. She knew it was a temporary deal on paper, but she could not imagine Bionamic letting go of a resource easily. If Max offered Darius a new exciting project after this one, she was sure he would be very tempted to accept. She had no idea how she would react if that happened.

When they moved the celebrations to a nearby bar, she was already trying to think of ways she could make her excuses, but was unable to come up with anything convincing.

When she spotted Scott Guest sitting on the other side of the room looking vaguely bored with the people around him she was surprised and delighted. She waved at him and he looked her way, his eyes widening. She was confused when he didn't smile in recognition but just shook his head, then gestured furtively towards the back of the bar, where the toilets and payphones were located. She excused herself to Melanie and tentatively followed Scott who had left his own group and was walking away without glancing to see if she was following.

When she reached the payphones she noticed a door leading out of the bar. Going through it, she found him sitting by one of several tables in the small courtyard outside. The relative chill of the evening meant that they were more or less on their own, with the exception of a couple making out in a corner.

"I can't believe you're here tonight!" Scott said as she sat down opposite him. "I was going to come visit you tomorrow."

"At the bar?" she asked.

"At your apartment," he replied. "I heard about your new job and a friend helped me dig up your address."

"You came all the way down here just to

visit me unannounced?"

"Well, officially I'm here for a wedding," Scott replied. "A guy from work—well, his sister actually—she's just tied the knot. So he's using their empty house as the base for a weeklong party while they are off honeymooning. He kind of talked me into it." Scott shrugged. "So, you finally gave up on the west coast then, Kim?"

"Yeah, I left years ago. No prospects."

"And Geoff?" Scott continued.

She sighed and looked down at her hands. "Like I said, no prospects. So how are you? It's been a long time. You still in New York?"

Scott nodded.

"You look great," she said.

"Thanks, so do you."

"How's work? Whatever work is these days."

Scott looked away. "Not so great," he replied. "I got hired by an electronics factory. It's really repetitive stuff and sometimes I think I'm going to die of boredom. I keep meaning to do something about it but it pays pretty well and I can pay the bills working only part time, so even though the hours are long, the actual workweek is short. Sunday nights, Monday nights, and half a day on Tuesdays. It leaves me some time for my. . .hobbies." He took a swallow from the beer he had brought out with him. "So how about you? How's work at Sytek?"

"Sytek is excellent," she said, wishing she had thought of bringing her own drink. "It's long hours and long weeks, but the work's interesting. I get to play with some fantastic equipment." She grinned. Back when she used to hang out with Scott and his group of computer enthusiasts, they had carried on conversations that went late into the night about the kinds of computers and machines they hoped to one day get their hands on.

"That's good," Scott said, but he wasn't smiling. She could sense that he was working his way up to something else.

"What is it?" she asked.

Scott looked at her. "And Bionamic?" he asked. She didn't reply. "We used to be against that sort of thing, Kim. Remember when we would hack the shit out of companies like that?"

"Yeah," she said finally, looking steadily into his eyes. "Remember when we were almost tracked down by the feds?" This time it was Scott's turn to be silent. Despite the fact that they had all escaped unscathed, the incident had signalled an end to Kim's association with the group of hackers. Some of the others, including Scott, had made an attempt to go on, but as far as she knew they had never worked up the nerve to do anything big again.

"Yeah, well. That was a long time ago. I hope we are both older and wiser by now," he said. Then he smiled again and shook his head slowly. "I can't believe I ran in to you like this. I knew it'd be an unusual week as soon as we arrived, when we saw this big guy, stark naked, running along near a church, carrying a bicycle he'd been handcuffed to."

"Seriously?" Kim couldn't help but laugh at the mental picture. "Welcome to D.C."

"Never did find out what that was about." Scott was grinning at her as she struggled to suppress her giggling. He had once told her he liked her best when she was laughing. "So you have no reservations about working with Bionamic?" This time he had the decency to look ashamed at bringing the conversation back around to the topic.

Kim sighed. "Of course I have reservations, but what can I do? This project is way too big to say no to. It doesn't help that it's interesting as hell and that I am actually excited to see how well it works. Do I wish we were doing it on our own with no multinational looking over our shoulder? Sure. Can we do it on our own? Not a chance. The things Bionamic have managed to cook up are so far ahead of us that they might as well be from a different planet and they have resources we can only dream of. Besides, I am not calling the shots here. Darius is."

Scott seemed to be studying her, perhaps trying to figure her out. "Look, this isn't what you think it is, Kim," he said. "This isn't the old Scott thumbing his nose at authority for the hell of it. I have specific reasons to be nervous about Bionamic that have nothing to do with the fact that they are a big multinational with as much power as the pope and the same tradition of infallibility. I don't know how much they've told you about how they came up with the technology you're helping them test, but I'm betting that it's less than the whole picture."

"What do you mean?"

Scott hesitated. "You know as well as I do that there are rumours out there about Bionamic."

"Sure," Kim said, rolling her eyes. "Rumours. Most of them are on the same sites that tell of the secret headquarters of the New World Order hidden beneath the Denver International Airport and how the moon landing was a big hoax."

"Yeah, I know better than to take that kind of thing at face value, but if you dig around a bit, you find out some strange things. Did you know that Bionamic paid the Burmese government the sum of 7 million pounds in 1982? That's no rumour, that's a fact; there's an official transaction record at the Central Bank of Myanmar. That was more than 12 million dollars back then. With inflation, that's an even slightly more astounding pile of cash. So for this amount of money you'd expect them to get something pretty special right? Like trade agreements or something. You know what they got in return?" Kim just shook her head. When Scott got going like this, you might as well just hang on for the ride and keep the questions for the final destination. "A box. An antique carved box, but still just a box. What kind of a box is worth 12 million dollars to a pharmaceutical company?"

Scott reached into his pocket and produced a

small notebook. From between its pages he brought out a folded piece of paper. He unfolded it on the table between them, smoothing out the creases. It was a printout of a photograph. In the picture was a carved chest with inlaid panels. The box was on some sort of stretcher and was partially covered by a piece of tarpaulin, but she could still make out symbols on the inlaid panels and along the edges.

"So the Burmese sold Bionamic a fake antique?"

"It's not a fake."

"It must be. That symbol there is clearly a representation of a DNA spiral, and these symbols here are mathematical annotations of some sort. It has to be fake unless—"

"Unless?" Scott encouraged.

"Unless the ancient Burmese were visited by aliens or something."

"Or something," Scott agreed. "This is an official photograph taken in seventy-four. I haven't been able to track down people who can decipher all of what's on there and even if I had, I am guessing it would take several years. But I have shown the picture to a mathematician who swears that part of it is expressed in binary."

"So what? The ancient Chinese used a binary system for the I Ching. The notion of something being either on or off is a pretty basic idea. It was definitely around in 1982. Even if your photograph is genuine, we are talking 1974 and both those ideas were well-known by that time."

"Yeah. Sure. It could be a fake that the Burmese government put together to sell to some gullible collector. There are only three things wrong with that. One: the expedition that found the box is documented. It was led by a retired British Army major who described the box in some detail, or what he saw of it before the Burmese confiscated it. Which means that if it is a con, it's the longest con I've ever heard of. Show a British private citizen the artefact in 1974 and then sit on it for eight years? Not likely.

"Two: it's just unnecessarily complicated. Why go to the trouble of embedding coded mathematical notation and representations of human DNA when you could just put any random symbols that don't mean anything and sell it to a private enthusiast?

"And three: while I have all sorts of negative associations when it comes to Bionamic, one

41

thing they are not is stupid. I don't see them shelling out that sort of cash without first verifying the chest is what it actually appears to be."

Kim sat silent for a while and just looked at the photograph. Finally she sat back and crossed her arms. "Fine. Suppose I buy the idea that Max Kohler bought a piece of ancient unknown scientific notation, on a chest of all places, for a lot of money. What's so bad about that? They are keeping it to themselves sure, but that is what companies do. That's how they make money in the end. By knowing something others don't."

"Even to the point of keeping it from their partners?"

Kim shrugged. "If I had gotten my scientific secrets from an ancient hope chest I might be a bit reluctant to mention it to others, too."

"Okay. I'll concede that point to you, but you have to admit that it's strange. That's not the only reason I'm wary of Kohler and his company though. You don't remember Frank do you? Frank Moretto?" Scott asked. "No, well maybe I never got around to introducing you to him. He's a good bit older than we are, so it felt weird bringing him to our meet-ups. Anyway,

Frank works for himself. He's an electronics engineer. He taught me a lot when I was younger. He introduced me to his friend Susan."

"Is this all going somewhere, Scott?"

"Well, yeah, as a matter of fact it is. England. Which is where Sue used to work and also where her uncle lived. Look, Sue, me, Frank, and Finley all hang out together."

Finley, Kim remembered, had been part of the old gang, a slightly strange but pleasant boy.

"About a year ago," Scott continued, "Sue doesn't show up to one of our get-togethers and she doesn't call or anything to let us know why. We try to call her but no one answers her phone, and we get a little worried, right? So we go over to her place and we find her going to pieces over her uncle who has disappeared. She says he's been kidnapped but that the police won't believe her."

Scott paused and leaned a bit forward lowering his voice slightly. Despite herself, Kim got drawn in by the conspiratorial nature of the conversation and leaned in to hear him. "Turns out he's been working for Bionamic. They say he's just secluded in one of their laboratories to finish some important work and cannot be contacted. Sue knows something is wrong though, because she'd been getting a letter from him every month up until they just stopped coming, and he didn't mention anything about it to her in any of them. It's been a year now and he has still not contacted her."

"I've heard about this I think. Professor Young? Was that his name?"

Scott nodded. "Yeah, Melvin Young. And he's not the only one. Other people working with, for, or against Bionamic have disappeared over the years. They never got any attention in the press. The only reason you've heard of Young is that Sue made enough fuss over there for it to reach us over here."

"That must have cost her a lot," Kim said.

"Well, she can afford it. She's done quite well for herself working in the computer industry. Well enough that most of her money these days comes from renting out luxury apartments she's fixed up from nothing, so she has a lot of free time to devote to personal projects."

Scott looked around the yard and Kim followed his lead without knowing why. The couple was still making out on their bench in the corner but otherwise they were still alone in the courtyard. "We even have an eyewitness. Well, sort of," he continued. "One of Sue's work colleagues over in England, a physicist by the name of Judd, saw them. They stopped him when he was out walking his dogs late one night."

"Who did?"

"Two men in a car. They wanted to know if he'd consider working on a special project with them. That's all they said. He refused, of course."

"That *is* strange," Kim agreed. "So what about Sue?"

"It was only when her uncle disappeared that they thought things might have been more serious than they first suspected. Judd was widely regarded as a problem solver, a doer, the sort of person you'd want on the team, especially if you were in the business of trying to open a quantum internet, or whatever else it is."

"So you're saying these people were whisked away to work on this internet? Why kidnap them? Why not just hire them? And how do you connect these people to our project, and how does the box fit into this whole thing?"

"Well, for starters, Sue remembers her uncle

talking about his work before he disappeared. He mentioned quantum entanglement and something he called resonance feedback."

Kim was momentarily lost for words. "She actually said resonance feedback?"

Scott nodded. "Do I take it this is ringing a few bells for you? Maybe you could confirm one or two details for me. I know somebody who'd like to know the truth."

Kim halted her careening thoughts for a moment. She knew if she continued down this path she would most probably be caught up with Scott and his friends again. She also risked alienating Darius and losing her position at Sytek. She wasn't sure she wanted either of those things.

On the other hand, this was a chance to find out what was really going on. Perhaps in time to save Sytek from becoming too involved with Bionamic. Finally, she broke the silence that had enveloped them. "Your friend Sue isn't the only one who wants to know the truth. Yes, I've got some details for you, alright. I'm betting they'll keep you and your friends amused for years."

"I'd rather they kept us busy," Scott said, leaning in even closer. "As in, following up leads."

"They might. Look, I don't buy everything you just told me, but I will agree that Bionamic is acting suspiciously. I'll help you find out what's happening. I want to know what we've gotten ourselves into."

Scott smiled broadly. "Really? That's great. I'd like to get you together with the others."

Kim shook her head. "If we are going to do this, we are going to do this right. I don't meet with anyone else. I'll talk to your friend Sue when I have arranged for a secure call. Once I do, I will give instructions on how we are to keep in touch after that—if I like what I'm hearing. I want to know what's happening, Scott, but I am not going to be one of your band of merry crusaders and I am going to cover my ass as much as possible. Now, where can I reach Sue?"

Kim thought she could detect a hint of shock in Scott's eyes as he wrote down Sue's telephone number. She had never spoken to him that way, never taken charge like that before. She was surprised to find that she liked it.

THREE

I

New York, Franks 20.30hrs

"Remember, keep down the noise, okay?" Frank said as Scott and the others seated themselves in his basement workshop. It was a unique room with an obscured entrance from the hallway above. The space was usually cluttered up with equipment of various levels of obsoleteness that Frank kept around because they might come in handy someday, and usually some sort of current, half-built project spread out on the desk and workbench. "Maria thinks you guys are going to get me into trouble. The less she is reminded of your being here the better."

Maria was Frank's wife. She hadn't been

around in the glory days, when they got up to real trouble, but she had heard enough of the stories to see them as a danger to the quiet home life that she preferred. They probably should find some other place to meet, but Frank and Maria's house was conveniently located for all of them and there was the probability that if they met somewhere else where Maria couldn't keep an eye on Frank, she'd object even more.

Finley was already seated in the massive beanbag he had once brought over for that purpose and Frank didn't like when anyone else used his office chair, so Scott settled into the faded leather two-seater along with Sue.

"So, what's this all about, Scott?" Frank asked when they were all seated, casting nervous glances at the staircase leading up to the house. "Your message said you and Sue had managed to locate your old pal, the one working at Sytek."

"You've talked to Kim?" Finley asked.

"Yeah, he met up with her in D.C. and Sue talked to her on the phone yesterday." Frank said. "Didn't you read the message?"

"Not all of it." Finley shrugged. "How is she?" he continued, turning to Scott.

"She's fine. A little uneasy about working

alongside Bionamic, but I think we can all agree that that's only natural."

"So what did she say?" Frank looked from Scott to Sue and then back again.

It was Sue who answered. "She told us a lot of things about their setup at Sytek and what Bionamic had told them. She's going to give us a memory stick with all the important details at a later meet-up with Scott. I don't know her as well as Scott and Finley, but she seems to be on the level. She'll help us as long as we direct our efforts at Bionamic and leave Sytek alone as much as possible."

"Okay," Finley said. "So how are we going to do that?"

"We hack the connection," Scott said.

Frank frowned. "Hack a quantum entanglement? Well, that should get us the Nobel prize at least."

"Not the entanglement itself; well, not the way you are thinking anyway," Sue explained. "We'll need to connect to one of the fibre-optic leads that's been laid down for these quantum internet tests. We located an empty house in Washington that's right near one of their main lines. Once we're settled in and there's an opportunity, Kim will send us one half of an entangled particle cluster from their back-up machines. If this is done carefully, the others won't even know the particles are gone. That'll give us a direct feed into Bionamic's side of the network. Hacking from there into Bionamic's systems is up to you guys."

"Is she going to get us one of their storage systems as well?" Finley asked. "Or are we just gonna keep the particles in a bucket?"

"For obvious reasons," Scott replied, rolling his eyes at his friend, "she can't just carry off one of their containment units, there's only one on this side of the Atlantic anyway, but she will give us the specifications and instructions on how to build one. Apparently Bionamic has been quite generous with their technical specs."

"We're going to *build* a photon trap?"

"Well. Frank is."

"Me?" Frank exclaimed, shaking his head. "I don't like it. This is Bionamic we're messing with here. If they demand action, the feds are going to jump up and pay attention. If they catch wind of us, we can't just lay low and wait it out. They'll keep looking until they find us. Are you sure it's worth that kind of risk?"

"People have been disappearing, Frank. The media have been suppressed," Sue remarked.

"Somebody at Bionamic obviously thinks something is pretty damned important."

"And there is more at the bottom of this, Frank." Scott leaned forward in his seat, eager to convince Frank of the need to act. "They haven't been coming clean with Sytek. They've told them nothing about the Burmese artefact and nothing about the earlier experiments. They are hiding something. Something big."

Frank sighed and threw up his hands. "Even if you are right, even if Bionamic is kidnapping people and browbeating the press, even if they are keeping secrets that should not be kept, what can we do about it? I can't build a particle storage device. I haven't got the equipment and I haven't got the materials. Most of all, I'm not a physicist. I doubt I would understand half the instructions."

"I'll help you," Sue said. "And I'll pay for any equipment we need, and all the other materials. I realise this is mostly my crusade. Scott has his own reasons for going along with me, but this started simply because I want to find out what has happened to my uncle. If I can find him, maybe I can save him. Or at least I can learn whether there is anyone left to save."

"It's not that I don't want to help you, Sue.

It's just that someone has to be the voice of reason here. Maybe there's some other way to find out?"

"Like what? Going down to Coney Island and asking one of the psychics?" Scott felt he was letting his irritation get the better of him and forced himself to calm down before continuing in a more pleading tone. "Look, Frank, aren't you the least bit excited?" Scott asked. "A chance to come into close contact with an actual quantum entanglement and you pass it up? This doesn't sound like you."

"He's right," Finley said. "It doesn't. What's the real problem, Frank?"

Frank sighed audibly. "I don't like the idea of going off to Washington. What am I going to tell Maria? She's upset enough with me as it is. Even without that, the whole damned thing is just a little too surreal. Waiting in that house you were talking about for the signal. For how long? I mean, an opportunity might not show up for days."

"We can take your pipe and slippers along if you'd like," Scott teased. Frank guffawed involuntarily but still looked a bit hesitant.

"We'll be renting the house, Frank, so we're not going to be in hiding or anything," Sue said.

"I've got an old friend who lives in the city who's got all sorts of connections and he's promised that he can get us some fake ID's. Our real names won't have to be on the rental agreement. He can even arrange some local transportation that won't be traced back to us."

"We've decided we're doing this, Frank," Scott said. "Only thing you need to do is decide if you're helping or not."

"I'm in, I'm in already! Like I'd get a moment's rest otherwise. Just one thing though," Frank added, now staring up at the ceiling and his home above. "You are all going to have to help me keep this from Maria."

II

Darius looked out over the drum and sighed. It was all coming together beautifully, but somehow he didn't feel as fulfilled by it as he normally would. Basically, he guessed it was because there was nothing really for him to do, other than to supervise things. The research they had been doing before had all been basic stuff, nothing that anyone would pay the big bucks for, but at least he had been involved in making the basic decisions. This time around, the actual project was absolutely fascinating, but all the big decisions were being made for him. It made him feel useless somehow. Superfluous.

He leaned on the railing, nodding at Ray and Dave as they left the lab. Potter was still at his station but he was packing up his equipment and getting ready to leave as well. Darius was glad to see them go home, especially Potter who had been spending all too many of his nights here in the lab analysing the resonance feedback from the entanglement and calibrating the interface device. Darius had been starting to worry that the man would collapse from overwork and had ordered him to go home at a reasonable hour. They had both stayed late, but eight pm was at least better than midnight.

The only other people in the building, once Potter had left, were Igor and Kim. Igor was waiting along with him for a videoconference call from Max, which was due any minute, and Kim had said earlier that she wanted to go over the packet loss statistics again. He was a bit worried about her too, but in a more personal way. She had become increasingly more distant as the project went on. In many ways, she was an idealist and working with Bionamic chafed at her in ways he couldn't fully understand. Since he had hired her, they had grown to become friends, united in their passion for science, technology and bad sci-fi movies, but their difference of opinion over Bionamic had put a barrier between them that he didn't know how to break down.

Others in the team had also been asking pointed questions about the way in which Bionamic chose to run things and the way they filtered the information that was handed down to Sytek, but their dislikes were more tangible. Whenever he talked to Kim about it, he kept ending up in dead ends where she wouldn't tell him her reasons for distrusting the multinational. He was getting the feeling that it was some irrational authority-defying principle she hadn't shown before, but it seemed out of character for her. He kept thinking that there must be something more to it. If only she'd let him know what it was, perhaps they could straighten it out.

Darius turned away from the drum, and where Kim was still sitting on the other side of the room, the light of the screen illuminating her features. Returning to his office, he found Igor already there and the conference equipment up and running. Before long it indicated an incoming call and Igor hit the accept button.

Max was sitting in an armchair with a half-full brandy glass on a nearby table. He smiled amicably at them and lifted the glass in a toast.

"I hear things are going great for you over there," he said in the way of greeting.

"Yes," Darius said. "There are some packet losses that we are trying to account for, but odds are they're not due to the entanglement but rather some undetected weakness in the equipment or the software. We'll get it sorted and then we can get down to the real science."

"Good. Good." Max took a sip of his drink and put the glass down. "I'm hearing similar things from our technicians here, so that would suggest a software problem of some sort since we are working with different hardware configurations, unless the problem is in the IPAS communication protocols of course. You do your analysis and then by the end of the week we can exchange information and correlate each other's data independently."

"Right. I'll tell our people."

"Oh. Before I forget. Some of my people were curious what your lot made of that resonance feedback effect."

Darius exchanged a brief look with Igor who replied in a surprised voice. "Is it important? I thought that wasn't part of the project."

"Oh, it isn't." Max waved his hand dismissively. "They're simply curious and I like to indulge curiosity when I can. They'd be excited to hear of anything you find out, I'm sure of it."

"Well, I haven't been paying much attention to it myself, and it is personal research so I can't force them to share it," Darius said. "But I'll let them know you guys are interested. In fact, I have a request from Potter to communicate with one of the people involved in studying the effect on your end."

"Really?"

"Yeah. There is mention of a professor Young. He seemed to be involved in creating the interface device and Potter is intrigued by some of his notes. He was wondering if he could talk to the professor directly and discuss his findings."

Max rubbed his chin with his hand thoughtfully. "I don't think that's possible, no.

Professor Young is unavailable at the moment."

"Potter thought it might be Professor Melvin Young. There was some story about a kidnapping?"

"There is no truth to that. His niece was stirring up trouble because he was getting to be too busy to send her postcards, but that's all it was. Professor Young is involved in top secret research and has been sequestered to help him complete it." Max frowned. "I didn't take you for the kind who listens to ugly rumours. We're both men of science, so let's keep to the facts."

"Alright. Facts. So how about some more facts about the science? We've been looking through some of the early experiments and there is no mention of where the original data for the experiments come from. Some of the theories you test seem to have sprung from nowhere. Are there even earlier experiments that we have no documentation on?"

"I'm not sure I like your tone. Bionamic has given you more than enough information for you to be able to manage your end of the connection. In fact, we have been quite generous. Suffice it to say that we have drawn from various different sources and some of those sources will be used in other projects which you are not part of and for which your staff has not signed a non-disclosure agreement. This is a cooperative project, not a merger. I'm sure you weren't expecting us to give you all our trade secrets."

"Of course not. They were simply curious," Darius said, deliberately choosing to echo Max's previous words. "And I like to indulge curiosity when I can."

There was a short silence where Max glared at them from the screen. "I can't hand over vital research documents without good reason. Still, if your people have some specific questions that can be answered by our scientists, I'll be only too happy to forward them. As to the resonance feedback research, I hardly have to remind you that since your people are analysing our property, the contracts explicitly state that any results of that research belong to Bionamic. Now if there is nothing else, I'd like to return to my guests."

The connection was broken before Darius could formulate a response.

The conversation with Max had worried Darius. Igor on the other hand had appeared cool and unimpressed throughout. As soon as the call was terminated, however, Igor started tapping at the keyboard of his computer, his former detachment replaced by a deep frown.

"What are you doing?" Darius asked.

Igor didn't look away from the screen. "I'm looking up Professor Young," he said.

"What, you think maybe he's got a blog?"

Igor gave him a disapproving look. "I am aware of the basics of the internet search, Darius. If that's your notion of helping, you might as well go off and get us a couple of coffees."

Darius grinned. There was no use getting in Igor's way when he got his mind set on something. "Right. I'll go get coffee."

In the line at the Starbucks across the street, Darius considered the conversation he had just had with Max. That Max wasn't telling them everything was obvious, but Darius hadn't really expected him to, and his attitude wasn't really so much unreasonable as unexpected. Much more like the head of a multinational corporation and not so much like the fellow scientist Darius had found him to be in previous conversations.

Only question now was if both the faces he had seen were part of Max's personality or if one of them was a façade, and in that case, which one was the real Max Kohler?

When he returned with the coffees, Igor was still completely absorbed by what he was doing and Darius contented himself with putting Igor's coffee on the desk beside him and then going to his own office to go through some of the administrative work he had been trying to avoid. Almost an hour later, he looked up to see Igor leaning back in his seat staring at the screen and stroking his beard.

Darius rose and opened the sliding door in the glass wall dividing their two offices. "So, how goes the hunt?" he asked. "Found the professor's homepage?"

"No, no website, Darius. I did find some mentions of him at different lecture tours but nothing more recent than four years ago. The place with the most information, strangely enough, is Bionamic's website. They have biographies of their scientists on there, and what looks to be a complete listing of Young's academic history. I also looked up a few of the books he is supposed to have written. All three of them are still being sold and advertised online. The author's information at the publishers gives us nothing new except for one rather strange bit of information that Bionamic didn't think to include. Apparently Professor Melvin Young was the founder of the ECSD."

"The what?"

"It stands for the European Commission of Scientific Discovery."

"Never heard of it. Have you?"

"Well, as a matter of fact, yes, I have. I remember them rather well. Everybody from my generation in the sciences will have heard of the ECSD. It all came to an abrupt end, and to my knowledge it was never fully explained why.

"They were mainly dedicated to encouraging exciting new research efforts, by handing out awards to up-and-coming scientists. It was a popular idea at the time, and the commission managed to hand out their awards three years in a row before disappearing. The rumours were that the whole thing had lost its funding. Now it would seem that perhaps it just lost its founder."

Darius considered it. "Maybe he didn't think it was important, or maybe he just forgot." He shrugged, realising how flawed his reasoning sounded. "Well, I don't know. Maybe he overlooked it because he had other things on his mind."

Igor shook his head in disagreement. "I don't like it. Remember what Potter said about the kidnapping rumours? Well, Max even admitted that there had been some sort of big upset about it, but when I search for any information about it online, even with specific search criteria, I get hits for twenty sites about other kidnapping cases before Young's name is even mentioned. It's like someone's gone through and bribed all the search engines."

Darius nodded. "While fooling search engines and messing with content on the web isn't impossible, it would take a very deliberate effort to do something like that. Why would anyone go to that sort of trouble?"

"But somebody must have," Igor persisted. "Even a search with the exact date and title of the first online article about Young's disappearance turns up an article series about young British painters and a series of images titled "The scientist as a child" before the actual article. I'm reluctant to cast any aspersions on our partners, but—"

"Well then let's not, for now," Darius interrupted. "I agree with you that not all's well in Kohlersville, but without Bionamic we wouldn't be involved in this project at all.

Before we do something that could impact the project I think we need a lot more facts. Bionamic is a powerful organisation, but I am not ready to suggest they have people dedicated to erasing the online information they are not comfortable with."

"Still, you have to admit it's strange," Igor said.

Darius hesitated then nodded briefly. "But then it's a strange world we live in, my friend. Anything's possible."

FOUR

As Kim sped north towards her arranged
meeting with Scott, a gathering storm ahead
darkened the evening sky. On the seat beside
her, in her handbag, was a thumb drive
containing the secrets of the entangled internet.
It had been almost too easy to go back to her
old ways. Making off with information she
shouldn't be removing had felt like slipping
back into an old comfortable overcoat. If she
hadn't been feeling so guilty at betraying Darius
and the others, it might have almost been
enjoyable. As it was, her hands were shaking
just a little from the tension even now, three
hours later. She was amazed that she had so
easily fooled the security logs into not keeping a
record of the information transfer. Had it been

too easy? She couldn't help thinking she had missed something.

As she left the freeway for one of the smaller roads, the massing clouds were looking dark and ominous. Keeping the speedometer at just above the maximum limit, Kim managed to pull into the diner's car park just as the sky broke out its first audible rumblings. She spotted Scott's Ford next to the door and sprinted through the falling rain to the entrance, managing to get inside without getting too drenched.

Scott was seated at a window table; a half-empty cup of coffee in front of him told her that he had arrived some time ago.

"I haven't eaten so I ordered some food. Did you want anything?" he asked her as she sat down.

She took a look at the menu and when the waitress came over with a burger and fries for Scott she asked for a tuna salad and a cup of coffee for herself. The waitress jotted Kim's order down on her notepad and then tucked the pen back behind her ear. A large bolt of lightning reflected off the windshields of the cars outside, lighting up the diner briefly.

"Wow! You're lucky you beat that storm,"

the waitress said, accompanied by a deep rumble of thunder. "It's almost right on top of us. You'd be soaked if you'd been a minute later."

Kim smiled politely at the waitress who walked back to the counter to call in her order.

"So how did it go?" Scott asked, taking a bite from his burger.

"At work? It was fine," Kim answered briefly, not really wanting to go into details. In fact, she didn't want to think too much about it at all. Of course she knew Scott wouldn't let it be.

"No problems at all?"

She sighed. "Not really. Everybody is too busy hunting down packet drops to worry about what anyone else is doing. Also Dave and Potter are totally engrossed in that virtual interface," Kim stressed. "You, however, will have to make do with a normal interface, unless you can build a pair of those goggles on your own."

Scott took another bite. "Well, I'm sure Sue would put up the money if she has it, but right now it's not a priority. Have you figured out why Bionamic are keeping you in the dark about their early research?"

"No. Either it's too valuable to be risked on us even with a non-disclosure agreement, or there is some other reason they don't want to share," Kim explained. "I don't think anybody really trusts them beyond the current project. Not even Darius or Igor, though they aren't exactly speaking their minds about it."

Scott nodded. "Frank is a little worried about the build and I think Sue is too, not that she's said anything. They're not fully convinced yet that they'll be able to manage, with the build I mean."

"They'll get by. It's not my field of expertise but Potter seems to think that the design isn't the hard part." There was another bright flash outside followed seconds later by a low rumble. "So what has your group been up to these past few days?"

"Not much. You could say we've had our mind on fashion." Scott chuckled briefly as if he had just told a joke. "We had a meeting at Frank's place after you talked to Sue and then we went over to her place Sunday night to make some preparations."

"Fashion?" Kim asked, confused.

"Finley threw a tantrum when Sue showed him the wig and the suit she wanted him to wear when they go to rent the house together."

"Right, fashion. I get it. So I take it nobody else has raised any objections?"

"Frank's a bit on edge, but that's just because of his wife I think."

Kim turned her attention to the storm. As she watched the raindrops splattering the hoods of the cars, she decided she could sympathise with Frank. She was feeling a bit apprehensive herself.

"Hell, Scott. What are we doing? Can you honestly tell me you've thought all of this through? Properly, I mean. I'm still not entirely sure why I'm risking everything for this."

"It's because of Bionamic, remember!" Scott responded, voice ascending. "And the way they think they can walk all over people."

"Right. That's almost every big business, though, isn't it?" Kim continued. "I've been asking myself the same question all day: Why am I still going through with this?"

"You're here though, and I...we appreciate it," Scott said. "I know it's all worth it for Sue. Look, I know you don't know her as well as I do, but I got the impression that you liked her well enough when you talked. This isn't just faceless people being affected here. At least not for me."

Kim nodded reluctantly and brought her mind around to the plan again. "Did Sue find out anything else about her uncle?"

"Not so much about him. She dug those wells dry back when it all happened. Young wasn't the only one who disappeared you know. Another guy by the name of Crane is rumoured to have gone to live in the northernmost regions of Scotland, but friends who have looked for him couldn't find him. A third, Lister, also went missing. Like Crane he was only ever spotted on rare occasions by people who just managed to catch an uncertain glimpse, you know, like an old neighbour, previous colleague, those sorts of people. Every now and then, someone would report having seen one of them in passing—never anything solid that could really identify them. And they were all scientists working in areas connected to Bionamic's research."

"That does sound weird. Have you found out anything else about them?" Kim asked.

"Very little, other than word of mouth. It almost feels like everyone but Sue was scared off or intimidated somehow."

"How do you mean?"

"Well, Young's disappearance was the only case the police investigated. We couldn't understand why they wouldn't bother looking into the other two. I mean, it's obvious they both went missing, there's no doubt about it. Frank seems to think it has something to do with mind control."

"Mind control?" Kim exclaimed. "Where'd he get that idea from?"

Scott shrugged. "Look, you're going to have to read between the lines when you sift through this stuff. There's some really strange things been going on here. Take the news about Young's disappearance. Aside from the TV reports, there were also several newspaper articles. When Sue went back to copy one of them for you, the page was gone. So being Sue, she started sniffing around. That's Sue for you —she doesn't let go once she thinks she has a grip on something. Anyway, she was convinced it was still there somewhere, only hidden."

"And was it?"

"Oh yeah. The HTML had been saved as screen dumps in a hidden directory. Just a load of gifs with numerical names referenced from a plain webpage that had been coded not to attract the web spiders. Like whoever took it down wanted to back it up out of sight so it could be brought back again at a later date."

"Like someone didn't quite approve of the executive decision to remove it, you mean?"

"Right. Someone wanted it gone and someone else saved it." Scott produced a clip-drive from his inside jacket pocket and pushed it across the table to her. "It's all on this."

Kim slipped it down into her purse and Scott looked at her expectantly. "You bringk sekrit plans?" he grated in a rather awful Russian accent. Kim slid the memory stick she had brought with her over to his side of the table without comment.

Scott paused, looking at it as if he didn't think it was truly real. "It's all on here?"

"Yes it is. You can trust me," Kim said. The words prodded Scott into action and the memory stick vanished into the pocket that had carried the clip-drive.

"I know," Scott said. "It's just hard to believe that I'm sitting here with solid information that the forum-dwellers on certain sites would give their right arms for. That was some of the stuff we discussed on Sunday. There's a lot of speculation going on about the quantum internet. In all sorts of places, too, not just the tech and science forums."

Kim nodded. She wasn't surprised.

"Do you think they could be right?" Scott asked, a gleam in his eyes.

"Could who be right?"

"Do you even go online anymore? It's all over the place. Some think that this quantum entanglement is creating micro-universes as it is being used, others say the information is going through some other dimension or that this is just what is needed to create a real net-realm, one you could actually travel to, well virtually anyway. There's even talk of it going through to some sort of alternate field or spiritual plane, like the Akashic Records."

Kim gave him a sceptical look.

"Look, all I'm saying here is that not everything on the internet is nonsense. This idea that we are about to achieve some sort of Cyberspace is growing in popularity."

"Yeah, well. Reality isn't a popularity contest. We deal with facts, Scott," Kim explained. "I'm a scientist, remember? That's what scientists do. As for being online, I don't really have the time or the energy to be on a million forums. I read my mail and sometimes I catch a TV show I've missed. Besides, I was never interested in the esoteric. If you wanted to discuss that kind of thing, you should have contacted Potter or Dave. They're always talking about weird stuff like that and then breaking down the scientific possibilities."

"So what *about* Potter and Dave? Do they think it's possible?"

"Do they think what's possible?"

"Accessing some sort of Cyber-dimension! Hitching a ride through time and space! From what you've told us, this resonance feedback could be a representation of some sort of three-dimensional space. Why couldn't it be something like that?"

Kim let her eyes wander around the room while trying to think of how to respond. This diner was old; it had seen better days but it was also welcoming, with a familiar smell of home-cooked food. "What do you want me to tell you, Scott? Together, the two of them know more about the brain and its signals than you and I ever learned, but if they seriously believe any of the stuff they talk about, they've never let on. If you want to know the truth, I think Potter is too busy wanting to imagine himself in a no-latency world where he and hundreds of other virtual people can float around cyberspace all day to fantasise about accessing some spiritual plane.

"He and Dave are examining this resonance feedback and trying to find out what it could be. I'm sure they are keeping their options open and not just going with the first idea that might fit the bill."

"And you? What do you think?"

"How the hell should I know?" Kim snapped. "Why is it you suddenly assume I know everything? You think once you work for one of the big companies that you're let into some big conspiracy?"

Their conversation was interrupted by the arrival of Kim's tuna salad. Scott looked right at Kim the whole time the waitress was there, and Kim sensed he was not satisfied with the answer she had given.

"Listen," she continued as soon as the waitress moved away to help other customers. "At the moment, we have very few firm facts and we are the ones working the technology. I haven't been involved in this resonance feedback so I couldn't tell you what it is. Dave and Potter have been spending all their evenings on it and *they* only have vague guesses. I'm pretty sure your forum buddies don't have a clue either." Scott finally looked down at his plate and she went on. "Forget about what you've read online, Scott. The only thing we can say for sure is that if the quantum internet works out, all our homes are about to undergo a massive technological upgrade."

Scott nodded, but Kim wasn't sure he was taking on board what she was saying. "By this time next year or the year after, who knows what advances will have been made, but I don't think a spiritual link is one of them. Any conclusion people from the outside make are going to be flawed since they don't have access to the research."

"So, what's your point? You don't have to be a scientist to have good ideas, you know," Scott said, sounding a bit indignant.

"My point, Scott, is that none of the official information being put out by Bionamic bears any resemblance to the internet rumours you are referring to. Meaning that unless they have better access to the inside info of Bionamic than we do, their 'information' is just idle speculation, hopes and dreams. None of the actual information about the resonance feedback has reached the public."

"It never will if Bionamic has anything to do with it. I just can't help thinking that this is something big and they're trying to keep it under wraps until they can make money off it."

"You might be right. I can't speak for anybody else at work, but like I said, I don't trust Bionamic any more than you do."

Scott looked at her in silence. Kim was almost starting to feel uncomfortable about the long pause when he smiled and started speaking again. "Why not come up to New York one weekend and pay us a visit?" he volunteered. "We talk about this kind of stuff all the time."

Kim just stared at him until he looked away again.

"Yeah, I know," he went on. "Minimum contact. Just never say never, alright? We wouldn't bore you, the theoretical implications of entanglement can keep Sue talking about physics for hours."

"Of course it will. And if it were all true, it'd be a huge deal," Kim agreed reluctantly, before trying to change the subject. "So, is that what you do now? Work, visit internet forums and hang out with your hacker friends? What's your life like these days?"

"Well, you know about work already—that's

a laugh a minute. I was seeing someone a few months ago, Rachel. She was alright. I couldn't get along with her friends, though. They were all about getting drunk, or high." He shrugged. "We still keep in touch, sort of, but I can't really say I miss her. To be honest, Kim, I'm quite happy with the way things are. Finley says hello, by the way. He hopes you're doing well."

Kim smiled. "What's his take on all of this?"

"Oh, well, you know Finley. He hasn't changed. Half the time he doesn't say much and when he does you don't know where he got it from."

Kim smiled. "Yeah, he always was one of a kind. He did have some wild stories, the kind of stuff that leaves you wondering why your own existence is so ordinary, really."

"Tell me about it."

"What was that thing again, the dream business."

"Used to say that somebody was trying to tap into his dreams. For real, I think! Apparently, he'd wake up in the middle of the night. In the beginning he had no idea why he'd awoken. After this had been going on for a few months, he came to realise it coincided with a car engine starting up in the street outside—no doors closing, just the engine, then the car would drive away. Anybody else would just think it was somebody off to work, unrelated, right? But not Finley. He swears that somebody, or something, had been hacking into his mind, into his dream. He said it was unnatural waking up in the middle of a dream like that, with his heart pounding. Oh yeah," Scott added, "remember too, that this only ever occurred on Feast days of the Saints, as marked on the calendar."

"That is a strange story. It's weird how Finley can say that sort of thing and you don't automatically think he's crazy. He seems to be so calm and collected, it doesn't cross your mind until much later that what he actually told you is just nuts." Kim turned to look out the window. "It looks like the storm might be ending." She added.

"Could be a nice drive home," Scott replied. "A few tunes, one or two smokes, a memory stick full of who-knows-what in the glove box."

"Are you going to be alright setting up the untraceable email accounts like I asked you to?" Kim asked.

"We've done it all before, remember?

Nothing's completely untraceable, but we've got a few fixes so traces won't lead to us."

"Good. So our future interaction is via these email addresses only. If you need some help, or have questions, send me a mail. I'll check it as often as I can. Oh, and I've selected the best areas to rent your house. The location of the optical line is drawn in on the close-up maps. It's all on the stick," she explained. "So, have we got any other questions, Scott? Are we missing any details?"

"Relax, already, it'll be fine. We're not ignoring the vulnerable situation you're putting yourself in at work for us. Frank was a bit worried at the slow pace we were moving at until Finley reminded him he wasn't the one who was most at risk here."

"I prefer not to dwell on it. You just worry about your end and let me handle mine."

"I've no intention of doing that, Kim. Neither has Finley for that matter. Let's just say we all appreciate the lengths you're going to for us; some more than others."

Kim smiled. She sensed that Scott and Finley had been discussing her circumstances at work, and for now, it was enough to raise her spirits. "You do realise that some of the materials you're gonna need are pretty exotic, don't you? Like ytterbium, for instance. Have you got any idea how difficult that'll be to find?" she asked, staring up at him. "You might want to try a few out-of-the-way college campuses. The scientific departments all have cameras these days, so you'd better be extremely careful."

"We know somebody," Scott quietly replied. Kim frowned and was about to protest bringing anybody else into the operation when Scott continued. "He's a good friend of Sue's. This is the guy who's getting hold of our IDs, and the van, as well as some other stuff. I think we're ready to set up the next bit. Don't you?"

Kim looked out the window and didn't answer. She was committed to doing this, but she wasn't sure that she would ever be ready.

FIVE

I

Finley thought it was interesting to note how Kim was slowly taking charge of the operation during the weeks after the second meeting between her and Scott. He had no problems with her calling the shots. She was the one in place at Sytek and as such, she was the one most intimate with the company and how they worked. She was also likely to be the first person to know if the hack was detected. Finley wasn't sure if any of the others had even reflected on the fact that they were now taking orders from the woman they had asked for help, but if they had, no one was protesting. Not even when she had insisted that the hack had to coincide with the lab's first full test of the network, giving them a rather tight deadline.

He guessed that along with her position she was also—with the possible exception of Sue— the most sensible of them all, and her instructions often ended up having the tone of sage advice. With her help, they had been able to build an outstanding looking IPAS from a small stainless steel pressure cylinder which had been cut in half, lined with the ytterbium in precisely placed groves, and welded back together. As to whether it would actually work, there was no way to know until the time came, but Finley felt pretty confident that it would.

Finding a suitable rental property had been more difficult, but in the end they had secured the perfect house. It was situated on a cul-de-sac, which meant traffic would be light, with Sytek's optic fibre line sharing the cable television run through the pipe-work serving the street. Behind the house was a large sloping grassy expanse, irregularly dotted by the odd clump of bushes and a few free standing trees, between them and the next properties.

The house had been rented using the false IDs provided by Sue's contact and they had spent the time between then and the day of the hack tearing up the floor to expose the PVC pipe that led the TV-cables into the house. Last he had seen the front room, there was a proper pit dug partway under one of the walls, and the bay window was being upheld by makeshift timber supports. It reminded him of an abandoned mine from an old western.

On the day Sytek was scheduled to run their test, Finley and Scott were on their way to the house in the newly camouflaged Ford Econoline van, Scott sitting in the passenger seat biting his lower lip while Finley drove. They had stopped on the way to obfuscate their vehicle's identity with a change of number plates and a few well-placed magnetic stickers and looked like any other local utility workers. They had also changed into grey coveralls to match the part. Sue and Frank were waiting for the van at the house, ready to receive Kim's signal to begin.

As they drew up outside the property, Scott jumped out and directed Finley into position. They then met at the back of the van where Scott picked up the traffic cones that would be arranged at the front and Finley erected a small canvas windbreaker next to the back doors.

When he was sure no one could get an unauthorised peek of their activities, he lit a camping stove and secured a pan of tar over it. Scott soon joined him carrying the shinny petrol-powered still-saw.

"Right, well, here goes it!" As Scott started cutting through the top layer of street, Finley grabbed a pair of crowbars from the back of the van and when Scott was done preparing a square of road surface, he moved in to pry the block out. Once the layer of asphalt was cleared, Scott set to with a pick and shovel, swiftly piling up gravel next to the hole.

The plastic pipeline came into sight a few moments later and they removed a top section of the pipe with an angle grinder at the junction where the cables for the house split off into a corrugated tube running in the direction of the front lawn. Somewhere in the loom of wiring they had now exposed to daylight was the optic fibre line they were looking for, as well as the television feed for the house. Finley jumped down into the street and crouched to examine the mass of wires as Scott climbed into the van.

"Pliers," he said, reaching his hand back over his shoulder. He felt Scott place the long-nosed pliers in his hand and rolled his head to loosen his shoulders. "Groovy. Time to turn the heat up."

"How tight is it down there?" Scott asked. "Is there gonna be enough room for the splice?"

Finley pulled a little at the cable and grunted. "I guess. It'll have to do. Actually it isn't too bad. There's more play in it than I thought." He reached his hand over his shoulder again. "Life-line," he said and was rewarded by a small metallic bracket connected to a wire line wound around a spool in the van. Laying down on his stomach, on a pillow that Scott had insisted they bring for comfort, Finley felt like he was going to slide forward into the hole. It was an awkward angle to work at, but after breaking the television cable running to the house, he managed to attach the bracket in place around the free end without much effort.

He pulled at the cable twice, signalling for Frank to haul the cable back into the house. The plan was to then replace the TV-cable with their own fibre-optics that led into their computer/IPAS setup in the house. Then they would just have to wait for Kim's signal before the really difficult bit was to start. Finley had been practising, speed-splicing fibre-optics for days now and he thought he could confidently say he was getting pretty good at it. Still, just the thought of it threatened to stress him out so he decided not to think about it just yet.

The cable end disappeared, along with the wire, slipping with surprising ease into the pipe leading to the house. He quietly wondered if Frank was lying sprawled on his back in the house now, the cable not having given him the resistance he expected. Finley couldn't help chuckling at the mental image.

"What's so funny?" Scott asked.

"Frank falling over," he replied. Before Scott could question this, there were two distinct tugs on the wire. "Time to bring it back home." Finley said as Scott pulled the wire back through the pipe, and along with it their own fibre-optic cable. Then he carefully lowered the fusion splicer from its resting place in the van. The splicer was a necessary piece of technology used to split and redirect optical signals. This machine was new, the latest model, capable of welding up to twenty-five lines simultaneously. Sytek's ten would be no problem for the machine; the challenge would be to splice all of them in the short time they would have.

As Washington went about its business, the

occasional car passing the cul-de-sac's end, Finley took hold of the end of the fibre optic cable that Frank had run through the pipe for him and fixed the individual fibres into place in one of the splicer's ports. Set into two of the other ports would be each side of the soon-to-be-severed quantum network cable. Finley then took hold of the quantum line and carefully wiggled it skyward. When he had teased several inches of slack line aloft he relaxed. Now there was nothing they could do but wait for Kim to give the signal.

* * *

At Sytek, things weren't running so smoothly. The setup for the testing had met with delays related with unexpected spikes in the noise to signal ratio. Kim was secretly relieved, she did her best to share in with the labs irritated mood, knowing Scott and the others would have plenty of time to be able to finish their preparations.

Sue had sent her a non-traceable mobile phone to use during the hack. She could send any number of prewritten SMS messages from it using shortcuts, communicating all the vital information needed to the corresponding phone held by Sue, with just a few keys. As soon as the lab tests started up, the message would go, and Finley would get the word to begin his part with the splicing process, when the systems would be booting up and the break hopefully would not be noticed.

* * *

"So what's taking them so long?" Scott's voice brought Finley out of his personal world of thoughts. Apparently Scott was getting anxious and had called up Sue. Finley could hear Sue's answer clearly even though Scott was sitting in the back of the van and Finley was still in position to cut the fibre optics.

"It'll happen when it happens. She warned us to expect a wait."

"Too dammed slow," Scott moaned, "I just want to get this part over and done with."

"Relax."

"Relax, she tells me? That's easy for you to say. I need something to happen Sue. This is like waiting around for an earthquake."

"Is Finley set?"

"You can tell her I'm set to stand up," Finley

shouted. "My back's starting to complain. It's telling me I'm not as young as I used to be."

"Listen to him," Scott joked, "25," he said staring down at Finley.

"I used to be younger. That is a simple fact, Scott."

"This is fast turning into an endurance contest." Scott said into the phone. "Finley's back is giving out and my mind is about to crack."

Finley stood up and stretched. "By the way, you might want to keep your voice down, if you don't want the whole neighbourhood to know what we're doing." He stopped talking briefly to roll a shoulder. "Damn. I think I found a new muscle I didn't know I had."

"It's your own fault. You should have stood up sooner. It would have been uncomfortable if we hadn't brought that cushion along."

"I was going through what to do in my head. Would you rather do the splice job, now?" Finley asked. "It isn't exactly straight forward. I have to get this right the first time."

"We have company." Scott watched the station wagon drive onto the cul-de-sac trying not to make himself appear suspicious looking. Finley peered at the car as it passed by then turned to see the vehicle come to rest on a nearby driveway. The occupants of the car were a group of noisy children and a woman who was most likely their mother. They'd been shopping and the mother was keen to get help with the grocery bags. They both stayed quiet as the woman got the children under control. As she gathered up some of her shopping, one of the elder children took an interest in the van. Finley could hear Scott swear under his breath as he made his way through the van. He crouched down behind the seats explaining that the youngster was watching. Glancing up at his mother the child took a few tentative steps towards them, only to be called away. Reluctantly the boy walked back to the car and picked up some bags.

"No, they aren't that concerned. Coast is clear. They're all heading inside, finally!" Scott explained with relief.

Finley couldn't hear Sue's response but Scott soon closed his phone, came back to the rear of the van and sat down, sighing audibly.

* * *

At Sytek, the hold-up was beginning to cause some friction.

"What are they doing over there?" Melanie asked loud enough so everyone could hear. As Kim made her way across to join the others, she could see Melanie was silently mouthing the same question to Tony who was standing on the lab floor with Dave and Potter.

"Why on earth do we have to go through this same routine every time we're testing something new?" she continued.

"It'll take all day at this rate." Kim replied.

"If it isn't one thing it's another," Ray joined in. "Anyone would think we were trying to launch a rocket."

Dave and Potter looked up at them and Potter held his hands up in a warding gesture. "I know I know," he uttered, "you've all been waiting for ages. This is just one of these things that you can't hurry. Not if we're going to get it right. In the end, it might not be anything important, but if these variations are caused by something in the hardware, we could fry some circuits and that'd only add hours onto the test time."

"Any longer, Dave, and it'll be time to leave," Ray joked.

"Ah, Ray, I'm afraid you'll just have to forgive my rudimentary understanding of quantum electrodynamics."

"What he's trying to say is, if we were still dealing with a more understandable particle interaction model," Potter interjected, not looking up from his work, "the adjustments might be slightly more straightforward."

"So, what you're actually telling us, is that you don't know what it is you're doing?" Tony joked.

"No," Dave replied. "What I'm telling you is, it's complicated."

Kim reticently wandered back across to her workstation and sat down without saying anything. She knew Scott and the others would be even more on edge than she was, but all any of them could do was wait. She settled in for a long delay and was almost caught off guard when Potter's voice could be heard five minutes later announcing that he thought they'd done it. As the system information began to flash on the giant display, signalling the system was booting, Kim quickly jabbed the four-digit sequence into her phone and a message sped off to Sue giving them the go sign.

* * *

Seconds later, Sue called up Scott telling him the signal had arrived. They'd decided to give it thirty seconds for the boot to be sure it was well under way.

"The way you've been obsessing about the splice for days now I would have thought you'd be more nervous." Scott told Finley as he closed the phone.

Finley shrugged and got down into position at the edge of the hole. "I can't do much more to prepare now. It'll either work or it won't. No sense in worrying over things I can't do anything about."

"Wish I had your Zen, man." Scott said.

"Not so much Zen, more like resignation." Finley joked. "How much longer we got?"

"Fifteen seconds. Fourteen, thirteen—"

"Just tell me when it's time," Finley replied. "Countdowns make me feel like something's about to go boom."

"Well, in that case, that'd be.. about... Now."

Finley, having put the cable cutters into position already, clamped down on the handle and snipped the cable, which came apart with a satisfying sound. Immediately he began to tease each individual fibre out from the line, deftly separating them all and attaching them all into the fusion splicer's loom. Finley could almost hear the alarm that would be going off at Sytek right now as his fingers danced to get the connection patched in time. When he finally hit the green weld button with a shaky thumb, he glanced at his clock and realised he had beaten his record from the practice runs. Breathing out, he anxiously lifted the splicer's plate to see how things had gone.

"Are you done already?" Scott asked from up above.

"I think so. It looks good, too. Just hope they're all in the right place."

Finley climbed into the van as Scott crouched down on the ground to inspect the results. "It looks perfect." He said, before spraying the exposed wires with a quick-setting foam gel. "I can't believe you did that so quickly. One minute I'm looking at you scratching the cable ends aside, the next...well, the next you'd finished it."

Finley smiled confidently and nodded from his place on the van's back step. "I have to admit, I wasn't expecting it to go quite so well. That really was fast. Guess practising really does work, after all."

"Take a break. You deserve it, Finley." Scott replied. "Well, hand me the pipe-lid first, then take a break."

Finley reached over and handed the cut-out portion of the PVC pipe down to Scott who quickly went about securing it into position. While Finley leaned back, looking up at the sky, he reflected that the sound of gravel being packed into a hole was a pretty soothing one. When Scott was done, they topped up the hole with some dirt they'd brought with them, replaced the square of tarmac, and poured hot tar which had been bubbling away in a pan on the camping stove, into the seams. Then they packed up the van and joined Sue and Frank in the house.

II

In the lab, Dave was already occupied by several automatically generated network reports. His confusion was almost palpable as he tried to account for the unsuccessful test and

Kim was trying to stay calm, while secretly waiting for him to give up so she could send the all clear to Sue.

Igor walked up next to Dave and leaned over his shoulder to peer at report printouts. "Did I hear you mention a polarity test?" He asked.

Dave shook his head. "It really makes no sense. Just look at this. There's been a massive cohesion reversal within the entanglement. But as for why!"

"So it is a reversal, then, confirmed?" It was rare to hear Igor sound as distressed.

"Just how much of a reversal, Dave?" Potter asked.

"Oh, about half. At least a third. According to these polarity parameters this sort of thing shouldn't happen. It shouldn't be possible. The overall efficiency of the system has dropped by almost eleven percent. Whatever caused that crash, briefly blacked out the entire network."

"Bionamic will be pleased." Potter replied.

"Can we," as Tony spoke his voice broke, "you know, rather than have to initiate another entanglement from scratch, can we reset it?"

"The whole system, or at least our side of it, has been corrupted by something, Tony. Before using the restore facility option we ought to try and find out just what has caused such a thing to happen first."

Igor frowned. "Eleven percent," he mused. "So is a straight forward reset an option, then, under these circumstances?" Dave put his mind to work, and Igor looked across to Darius, who was quietly contemplating the whole matter standing beside the railings over the drum. "If we were to trouble Bionamic with lengthy delays," Igor continued, "and this turned out to be nothing but a minor glitch, we might look silly!"

Darius waited for a second or two before responding. "I'd hate to have to bother Max with a delay." He said. "Okay, suggestions! I want to hear what everybody has to say. Ray?"

"Who would want to have to deal with an angry Max," Ray said. "But then, what are their people going to add to what we already know."

"Well I for one vote for a quick fix option," said Potter, briskly.

For some reason everyone focused their attention back to Dave as he was straightening his glasses. He then rubbed his head apprehensively. "Aw, heck. Let's just do that. We're getting nowhere like this. Just keep our fingers crossed, I guess."

With a nod, Darius had confirmed that the team should try the quick reset idea, a decision he would later regret. Inwardly, Kim breathed a sigh of relief and quickly sent the code to Sue which meant there were no immediate problems to worry about.

SIX

I

The next few days showed Kim that she had misjudged the reaction the failed network test would cause. Bionamic had been putting pressure on Sytek to do a thorough investigation into the cause of the anomalies that had been found. Darius had given Dave the task and Kim knew that between the pressure from Bionamic and Dave's natural inquisitive nature, he would not be giving up until he found out what had happened. Originally, Scott's group had planned on letting things cool down before receiving their half of the entangled particles. However, the increased attention meant that their window of opportunity was rapidly closing and Kim felt compelled to move the schedule up and notified Scott she'd be sending the particles on Monday.

Leaving work that afternoon, Kim had found herself wondering how much longer she'd be making this journey. If the hack was discovered, which she was almost certain it would be, she would be under scrutiny along with all of her colleagues. Scott and the others had not been happy about the change in plans, but she soon convinced them that if they didn't listen to her, their access to the particles might be gone before they had a chance to make the transfer, leaving them with nothing but an empty IPAS.

Frank looked at Sue as though he were lost for words. "You know what this means don't you?" He asked. "It means we'll be working on this IPAS, down here, from now until Sunday night trying to get it ready in time," Frank griped. "Followed immediately by a very long drive!"

"Look at the bright side." Scott said. "We'll be waving bye bye to Washington a lot quicker than we originally thought. As soon as we're through with the capital, it'll be straight back on the highway. You'll be home again before you know it."

"And it will be nice to finally have my own space again, but that's later," Finley said, trying to move the conversation onto more important matters. "What I want to know is if our escape plan is a go or not. With the system under scrutiny they're sure to notice this particle transfer, and with their own fibres they can use latency to locate us. So we've got to be ready to run."

During Scott and Finley's previous stay in Washington, the two had spent an afternoon tracing out a suitable escape route from the house should one be needed. Their pick up point, at a nearby mall, was a good five minutes drive, less at speed. The transfer itself would take almost no time at all, but before they knew for certain that their IPAS was working flawlessly, before they could make the final readings and calibrations that made sure that the containment was stable, they would not be able to move the IPAS. They had decided, in the event of any unforeseen trouble, that it made no sense for all of them to stay. One person could escape more easily than four, if it came to that.

Sue turned to look at Scott and Finley. "You

two decided which one's going to take the risks?" she asked them.

"I think so," Scott replied. "I'll do it."

"You sure?"

"He isn't," said Finley. "I'll do it. I'll use the Volvo, and you all can take the station wagon."

Finley studied the others' faces. He saw worry there; worry about what would happen to him if he failed to get away in time. In Scott's face he could also see relief. Relief that he had been let off the hook, plus maybe a little guilt as well.

"Are you certain you'll be able to manage this situation okay?" Scott asked, a half-hearted attempt at giving Finley a chance to back out.

"He'll manage alright," Frank said. "This is one area he won't have any difficulty with. The computers don't matter, they're untraceable, we won't need them back. Once you've checked that the readings are within the parameters that Kim sent us, it'll be as easy as grabbing the IPAS and unplugging it. Right, Finley?"

"Right," Finley agreed. There should be no problem. As long as they managed to make the last tests and adjustments to the IPAS by Monday, everything should be fine. He smiled at the others to show that everything was all right, but his insides were already churning. He couldn't help wishing Scott had been a bit more insistent, and was then disappointed in himself for feeling that way.

"Thanks for doing this," Sue added.

"Either way," Frank said, now staring at Finley with a glimmer of admiration, "you're a braver man than I."

II

It felt like Monday arrived with a clatter of activity as the group made some final adjustments to the IPAS only hours before the scheduled time for the download. Leading out of the living room, trailing beneath the door, a fibre optic cable wound its way across the hallway carpet and disappeared into an ever-more-cluttered-looking dining room at the back of the residence. From outside, they could hear the sound of the neighbours' cars leaving for their Monday morning bout with commuter traffic. The sunlight crept along the wall opposite the window as they waited with increasing anxiety for the download to start. Frank, in particular, was very fidgety.

"Go straighten out the front room, Frank, if you're stuck for something to do," instructed Sue. "At least it'll keep you busy."

"Yeah sure, I might do just that. Later," he grumbled.

Finley peered over at Frank. He had been in a strange mood all morning, quiet and subdued.

"Do something to distract yourself. Go and watch the TV," Sue continued, exchanging a glance with Finley and Scott, before they all turned to look at Frank. Finley thought his smile seemed forced as he nodded slowly and prepared to get up.

"Damn, Frank. Have you put kick-me signs on all of us or something? You're pretty antsy about something."

"Something wrong, buddy?" Scott asked.

"Why would there be something wrong?"

"Oh, I don't know. Perhaps because you look as if you've won five bucks after losing a grand."

"If there's something you need to tell us, Frank, now might be the time," Sue added. "I haven't seen you like this before."

Nervously rubbing his chin, Frank finally gave up his pretence. He turned to face Finley with a guilty frown. "You're right," he began.

"There is something on my mind. You know how we agreed it wouldn't much matter if we left this computer and everything else behind, if we were forced to leave in a hurry? Well, I kinda think it probably does matter now. In fact, I'd say it's gonna be essential that we remove it." He looked around the room nervously. "I'm sorry."

"What are you saying, Frank? Is this parts related? I thought the parts I got for you had taken care of that," Sue demanded, now looking very serious herself.

"I might have made a blunder. With the build. I say me; it was the children really. What happened was that they got into the basement when Maria was waiting for the car on Friday afternoon. They were playing around down there and knocked over that makeshift table," Frank lamented. "It was like a bomb had gone off . There was stuff all over the place. Cleaning up wasn't so bad, but I never wrote down which parts were the untraceable ones we got through you, Sue."

"Damn it, Frank. Why the hell didn't you tell us earlier? We could have ordered a new batch," Sue yelled. Finley thought it was the first time he had heard her raise her voice.

"There wasn't even nearly enough time to start ordering new gear, Sue. Look, I'm sorry!" Frank repeated. "I couldn't make you ask Kim to move the deadline," he continued turning to Scott. "We weren't planning on leaving the computer anyway, right, except in an emergency, so it might not matter. I thought it would be okay."

"I knew we should have waited," Scott complained. "I knew four days wasn't enough. I should have told Kim we weren't ready."

"I did my best to separate them all out again, but Maria got down there while I was scolding the little,,,, and started trying to straighten things out. She just managed to mix them up even worse, I think. Anyway, I might have sorted everything out. Might still be okay."

"But it might not," Scott said.

"Yeah. There again, it might not. Probably not. It'll only be a problem if they get hold of the actual machine, though, and take it apart."

"So its another item to carry then." Finley remarked. "It isn't as if we can do anything about it, so lets just stop worrying. I'll just have to lug it along with me, whatever happens."

III

At the lab, Darius was feeling the pressures of the day. They had encouraged Dave to continue his investigations into the troubles they'd had during their testing, since he was certain that there was something more to find out. Meanwhile, however, everybody else was getting increasingly anxious and irritated as the interruption delayed their work.

Now it seemed he was getting somewhere though; he was conferring with Igor in hushed tones, looking confident. Eventually, Dave hurried off and Igor turned to enter the office. Darius looked up expectantly.

"Dave will be joining us in a moment," Igor explained, closing the door behind him. "He's got something. He's not sure what, exactly, but he's telling me the cable company's engineers are a waste of time. He's just going over the last of his data."

Igor opened the door for Dave a few moments later when he came striding back across the lab clutching a single sheet of paper.

"Good news?" Darius asked.

"Actually, it is."

Darius eyed the paper in Dave's hand. It was

some kind of map on which he had made several markings with a highlighting pen. "The monkeys at the cable company said there was no way of doing this. All I can say is they're not trying very hard. It was outside interference, alright. I'm sure of it. Anyway, this map will show you what I've got." He handed Darius the paper. "That's a print-out of Annandale. The network follows the streets I've marked. As far as I can make out, the line was broken right...there," Dave said, leaning over to point out the exact spot.

"Right where this cross is, you mean?"

"Obviously we have no idea if it's connected to that exact house, of course, but it seems likely. That's the one closest to the line break."

"So how did you conclude where the break occurred?" Darius asked passing the map on to Igor.

"Well, there was no sign of any trouble other than that one break in communications along the delta line. That in itself was more than a little suspicious. So I asked myself, assuming that I wanted to get access to our fibre optic network with as little disruption as possible, if it would be feasible to do so with anything currently on the market today. Next stop was contacting a few splicer manufacturers to talk to them about specs."

"This'll be interesting. What did you find?" Igor asked.

"Well, there are definitely a couple of fusion splicers out there that could make such a job possible, but they'd have to be very good. I didn't have any way to prove there was any such disruption made, though, without digging up half the city. Until I realised we had been recording all traffic between the cable company and the lab since the start of the trials. I went back through and compared those to our current traffic rates, as well as all the traffic data for the day of the disruption, and I was able to get an approximate location of where in the line the break, suspected line break, probably took place."

"Excellent. This is why we asked for your help," Darius added. "Igor and I both felt it'd suit your skills."

Igor opened his mouth to speak and Darius could tell he and Dave were about to launch into further discussion of technical details and interrupted them before they could begin.

"Call the cable company. Tell them what we've discovered. And then let's grab a van and head over to the area of the break to do a little surveillance work of our own. Dave, you're with us."

"But, shouldn't we call the police?" Asked Dave.

"Let the cable company concern themselves with that, if they want police involvement, they can arrange it." Darius didn't have much time for the cable company anyway. This matter served to confirm his opinion of them. He wanted to get to the bottom of who might have performed this hack.

Igor gave Darius a surprised look. "Isn't this a bit risky?"

"I'll be damned if I'm going to sit by and watch someone make an attempt to sully my company." Darius could feel himself beginning to seethe now. He hadn't realised how much this angered him, but he genuinely felt defensive about Sytek and all the work he'd put into it.

He marched out of the room on his way to the parking lot, and just paused outside the door to add, "If these hackers want to spy on us, why can't we turn the tables on them?"

IV

At ten a.m, when the signal came through from Kim, Sue acknowledged the connection on their end. In microseconds, their consignment of the entangled particles had arrived. She was heatedly shouting out Kim's warning for the third time as they were finishing up. Finley could see Frank's hands shaking until he had made certain that everything was okay.

"At least I haven't messed up this part for you," Frank told Finley, before once again going over the correct order in which he was to disconnect the computer and IPAS from the network. "It's in there. Whatever it is. All you'll need to do, Finley, is let the computer go through the program and calibrate the rest of the settings before you can finally pull all the wires. The numbers you need to compare to are on the paper that Sue gave you. That's all you'll really need,, here."

"Right, I've got it. You'd better get going hadn't you?"

"Let's go." Scott shouted, and Sue closed her laptop.

"I'll start loading the car," Sue responded.

Frank turned back to Finley in an attempt to be reassuring. "We'll be waiting for you, exactly like you and Scott arranged."

"Yeah, don't even give that a second thought," Scott added.

The house was transformed into a hive of frantic activity. Frank, Scott and Sue carried things out to the car while Finley studied the list of numbers he had been given, comparing it to the numbers on the screen, going over their relationship again, even though he had done so several times already. The activity soothed him. In the corner of the screen, a window was displaying a cloud of green dots that winked in and out of existence, rotating slowly around its axis.

"What is this?" He asked Sue as she came in during her final sweep of the house, looking for anything that could be traced to them.

"What's what?" she asked, only glancing briefly in his direction.

"The green dots."

She came to stand beside him, staring at the screen. "I think..." she began. "I think it might be that feedback my uncle spoke about."

"There's nothing on the paper about it."

"I didn't know it would be here, now I

mean. Someone at Sytek must have added it before Kim copied the program for us. Just ignore it, alright." But Finley noticed that Sue lingered with him, reluctant to take her eyes off the phenomenon.

"Let's get those last things in the car!" Finley said, standing up. Sue looked away from the computer and smiled a little apologetically as if embarrassed by her fascination. He smiled back at her and they joined Scott and Frank who were on their way into the garage with a carry.

"Just keep your cool," Scott said meeting Finley in the hallway. "It doesn't matter what's going on out there you stay focused on what it is you need to do. We'll all be back in New York before night fall."

"That's right, man. Home free!" Frank said, still looking decidedly edgy, his cheerful tone frayed at the edges.

"As soon as you see the first sign of trouble out there, step on it. Don't hang around for nothing, Finley," Scott continued. "I expect they'll be more concerned by that road scar, rather than the house."

"It's just a case of disconnecting now," Sue said as she joined them in the hallway, indicating the living room. "Laptop and IPAS

115

only Fin, the cables are all off-the-shelf so don't even give them a second thought. And don't take any chances with your escape," She continued, brushing past them in the narrow hallway, giving Frank an irritated look.

Finley handed the last of the gear to Frank as Scott settled in behind the wheel of the station wagon. Frank rode shotgun and Sue climbed in the back seat.

"Good luck," Scott said, grasping Finley's hand firmly through the driver's side window.

"Yeah, good luck, Finley," Frank agreed, though Finley thought Frank was avoiding looking at him. *He's still feeling guilty; probably will until I make it out safe,* Finley thought. *Better make it out safe then.* Frank was worried about enough things as it was and Finley didn't want to be another thing on his mind.

"We'll see you at the mall," came Scott's final remark before he started the car and headed out.

* * *

Darius and Igor sat in one of the company's vans with Dave behind the wheel. They pulled into the small street where the break had to be, and spotted one of the cable company's work vans, and a pickup truck, parked near a portion of tarmac that did not match the rest.

"That looks fresh," Igor muttered. "It's hard to tell exactly, but if I had to guess, I'd say not more than a week old."

"No sign of the police?" Darius said. "I'm kind a surprised they're not here. Cable guys aren't wasting any time."

"The police could show up at any minute, then," Dave said. "I'll park up over there, on the other side of the road, just in case."

Darius climbed out of the van through the sliding side door. He wandered back and stared over at the house across from the patch of tarmac and frowned.

Igor joined him. "So, how do you intend handling this?"

"Like I'm expecting anything to happen."

"You also think we're being watched, do you?" Igor asked.

"It must have crossed their minds." Turning to acknowledge a cable company workman, who with his colleague were preparing to dig into the darker patch of asphalt, Darius spoke up in a louder voice. "Has anybody seen any movement in there?"

"Nothing," the manager said, and the others shook their heads in agreement.

One of them pointed to the tarmac. "We're gonna cut it open."

"Don't you need a permit for that?" asked Igor, looking worried.

"We have authorisation in case of emergency," the manager stated. "And reopening this hole is the only way we'll find out for sure what's been going on here."

"So just out of curiosity, did you happen to notify the police?" Darius asked.

"We did. Supervisor told me a unit was sent right away."

"Yeah, but remember this is D.C. right? They're always getting lost." One of the other workman snorted.

Over the next few minutes Darius felt his eyes being drawn towards the house across the street several times. Between that and wondering why Dave was taking such a long to join them, he and Igor both realised that they were here merely as observers. When the muffled roar of an engine fired up, the noise coming directly from within the garage connected to the house, all had turned towards the sound half expecting they knew what might be about to follow.

* * *

A slit at the top of the garage door had provided Finley with a good view of the cable van's arrival. He had been standing on the Volvo's bonnet watching the van's occupants apprehensively staring over at the vicinity of the house, before each shifted their gaze back to the road scar. Within moments, the van had been joined by a large pickup truck. Its fat driver had blocked the driveway, and sauntered over to his workmen with a laid-back attitude, tucking his shirt into his pants.

Finley's escape might have worried him had he and Scott not planned for a moment such as this. Now he was watching the unfolding scene with almost zen-like confidence. Since he couldn't hear any distinct conversation outside, he carefully stepped down onto the garage floor. Leaving the garage by the connecting door through to the kitchen, he disappeared into the back room and looked at the screen on the laptop. The process was almost complete, just a few more seconds. The green clouds in the feedback window also seemed more complete somehow, more accurate. He didn't know why, but that was the impression he got. He then ran upstairs for a better look at what was going on outside and soon saw a black people carrier turning into the street. The vehicle slowly rolled to a stop outside and Finley could see two of the car's occupants get out and begin talking with the work crew. Finley could see that the newcomers were not actually part of the crew, but nor did they seem to be police or FBI. Still, he couldn't take a chance. He went down and checked the readouts again. Everything seemed fine: the numbers matched the ranges he had on the sheet of paper. He should just pick up the IPAS and the laptop and go, but he found himself hesitating. The green clouds shifted in the little window but they seemed wrong to him, off somehow. He reached for the laptop and was about to disconnect it when he hesitated again. The clouds on the screen rotated and something clicked into place, suddenly they seemed exactly right. He didn't stop to analyse what had just happened, he just collected his things and ran to the garage.

With the bag containing the computer and

IPAS secured in the passenger seat of the car and the removable drive containing all the data shoved deep in a pocket, Finley hopped up onto the bonnet one last time to steal a final glimpse at the growing crowd outside. Then, he jumped down and got behind the wheel of the car. Quietly shutting the car door, he fastened the seatbelt across his chest. There was no going back. He fumbled with the keys before he got them into place. Ready to start the engine, Finley hit the garage door remote and prayed it wouldn't jam on the way up. When it was halfway open, he started the engine and hit the gas.

Smashing through the trailing bottom edge of the flimsy garage door, Finley watched it disappear above his head with a tinny thud. He immediately lurched the car left, skidding across the lawn and flattening the neighbouring property's fence with another loud crash. Some of the crowd down by the asphalt patch ran for cover, scattering like leaves in a breeze. Finley did a quick check in the rear-view mirror to see that no one had been injured in the resultant upheaval.

Only after rolling onto the cul-de-sac via next door's garden path, and after also having narrowly avoided hitting their car, did he hit the gas proper. The laptop had slid out of the bag and onto the floor during his manoeuvres, but there was no time to reach down and get it now. Racing towards the open road at high speed, he cut into traffic to a chorus of angry horn blasts.

Now caught up in the flow of traffic, Finley shifted his attention behind him. Nervously checking his mirrors, he caught sight of the black van surging out onto the larger road, bullying its way forward. Swearing, Finley swerved into the centre of the road as the other vehicles were beginning to slow down for a set of changing lights. Both vehicles careened through the intersection at speed, the people carrier narrowly avoiding catastrophe by veering suddenly away from an unsuspecting car.

Finley saw the black vehicle gaining on him and realised that despite being away from the house, he was far from safe. His only advantage was that he knew his destination and as the traffic thinned out on the other side of the lights, he took full advantage of the Volvo's hidden performance and carved out a bit of distance. His car was a good bit faster than the pursuer's and he increased his lead through the next few set of lights until one of them turned red just as he was closing in.

Hesitating for a second, Finley decided to ignore the red light and instead he gunned it through the junction and swerved onto the freeway access road. He ended up behind a trailer-hauling pickup whose driver was not inclined to make overtaking him easy, and the people carrier was near to catching him again.

In desperation, Finley attempted to squeeze through the narrowest of gaps and keep his distance. The side of Finley's car made contact with the pickup, and the other driver furiously pounded on his horn and veered to the right, which allowed the people carrier to pass unhindered. As both vehicles joined the freeway's heavy traffic, Finley realised the Volvo's extra power would be of little assistance to him here.

The two vehicles negotiated strategic lane changes on the fly, passing cars on both sides at an alarming rate. Finley was greatly relieved when he spotted his exit. Diving back between the traffic, and across two further lanes, he hurtled down the off-ramp before running yet another set of red lights. Emerging onto the city streets at a speed faster than he had ever cared to in the past, he was dismayed to see that he'd still done little to shake off the pursuer.

He headed for the area he and Scott had previously surveyed: a narrow back street between a row of shops. It had been converted to a pedestrian walkway some years earlier and led directly into a shopping arcade. As both vehicles rounded the final corner, Finley was still ahead but not enough for his purposes. Turning the wheel sharply, he ducked between the slow oncoming traffic and bounced onto the opposite sidewalk with an unforgiving suspension crunch, wedging his car across the back street's opening.

He grabbed for the bag with the IPAS and opened his door. He looked for the laptop but it had lodged under the passenger seat. No time left, Finely sprang out of his seat and out the door. He sprinted past startled onlookers and wove between the meandering shoppers at full tilt. Only after reaching the arcade's entrance did he bother to look back.

A small crowd were already gathering around the abandoned car. A few were still staring in the direction he'd taken. Only one person caught his eye though, the people carrier's driver, who was scowling straight towards him. Finley smiled at the man, doffed his baseball cap in what he imagined to be a cheeky manner, and calmly disappeared through the mall's entrance.

SEVEN

I

Darius watched the images on the computer screen closely. He had uploaded the photos taken on their trip, including a few pictures inside the house that he had managed to shoot before the police got there, and now he was studying them in detail trying to find anything that could tell him more about the people behind the intrusion into their network. The photographs confirmed his belief that the hack was not the work of amateurs and the circumstances of the operation—cutting the street open, renting a house right nearby one of their optical lines—made him believe this was not one man working on his own and also that

126

whoever they were, they must have had access to inside information from somewhere. He leaned back in his seat and closed the image program grating his teeth. Nothing useful had been left inside the house. There were a few chairs and a cheap table, but anything potentially traceable had been removed with them. The multiple chairs certainly indicated several people. And the fact that the driver Dave had chased through the city had only grabbed a small bag before leaving the car made it clear that all the other tools and computers must have left the house with someone else.

Through the glass wall, he could hear the indistinct voices of the others discussing the result of their outing. The story about what had happened had been met with some disbelief from those who had stayed behind. Potter in particular seemed to have a hard time believing Dave had actually been involved in a car chase. In the end, it had been the calm insistence of Igor that convinced them it was all real. As Darius opened the door and went out onto the observation ledge of the drum, the murmur of voices coalesced into clear words.

"You should have grabbed it when you had the chance," Potter was telling Dave. "It would have made things a lot easier."

"What was I supposed to do?" Dave asked. "Just make off with police evidence out of a wrecked car in the middle of a crowd?"

"Well I would have done!" Potter declared.

"Leave him alone, Potter," Melanie said. "I think he did very well as it is. I'd like to see you try chasing another car half way across town."

"It doesn't really matter anyway," Tony interjected. "Getting our hands on their computer, I mean. There won't be anything on it. They'll have been using a portable drive."

"Tony's right," Ray agreed. "These people are professional."

"What if he wasn't after information? What if his real intention was trying to get access to the entanglement?" Tony then asked.

"To study it directly? As in a competing company being behind all of this?" asked Dave, his tone making it clear that he disagreed even before his words did. "That doesn't make sense. It would take very specialised equipment to make any real research on the entangled particles, and the information you'd get out of it would be limited. Any competitor to Bionamic would get far more information by just getting their hands on the details of the IPAS, or

Bionamic's theoretical research, rather than actual examination of the entanglement. Either way, to be able to do anything remotely interesting, they'd need both sides of a pair and that'd be impossible to get from just our side. And even if they did breach Bionamic as well, which is a tall order, how do you separate out one specific particle to be the pair of one you got from us, that'd almost be more trouble than doing the research for yourself."

Tony shrugged. "I know I haven't studied quantum physics, not even in my garage," Tony grinned to show he was joking, but Darius noted that Dave still narrowed his eyes. "But shouldn't you be able to do something with access to one side of an entangled pair just the same?"

Darius interrupted before Dave could make a more heated comment. "Not if they were interested in the process of entanglement itself. Most of the research into this is in how to achieve an entangled state easily, and for more advanced or practically minded scientists and engineers, what to use it for. If you're looking for the first, you don't need the entangled particles; you'd want information on the method for entangling them in the first place

129

and then keeping them entangled. That would mean needing the IPAS, which you would already have to have in order to steal a particle in the first place, or the DUPO, which we don't even have access to ourselves." Having reached the bottom of the stairs he leaned against one of the machines under the walkway. "If you are looking for the second, then you need to be able to test the entanglement, read it, see how reliable it is under different circumstances. You'd need to be able to feed changes in on one end and then read the result at the other. That you can't do without both particles in a pair, at the very least. No, I'm afraid Dave is right. I don't think research is the motive here. With access to only one side, there is nothing really to research."

"Unless..." Potter spoke up, having been quiet for a long time. "Unless, they knew about the resonance feedback. That's something you can study with access to only one side."

"How could they?" Dave asked, hurrying the words in before he was cut off by Darius or Tony. "They would have needed inside information to know about that. Are you saying this whole thing was organised by some disgruntled ex-employee from Bionamic, or something?"

Potter shrugged his shoulders. "I'm not suggesting anything of the sort. I'm simply saying that it's something that can be studied without access to both ends of the entanglement."

Melanie shook her head. "I really doubt it. They're probably just a bunch of local college kids who are daring each other to see if they can be the first to hack into the quantum internet."

Potter raised an eyebrow. "To the point where they decide to rent a house in the suburbs to do it? I can see college kids doing it out of their school's computer lab, but this kind of thing? I don't think so."

Darius felt that the speculations had gone far enough and decided to end the discussion. "Before we start listing every possible scenario, let's just stop and examine the facts. Unless we get our hands on that computer, we won't learn anything more about the guy Dave was chasing. What we *can* do is make sure that there isn't any foreign code left in our system, or that anything we don't know about has been messed with. We'd better go over the entire thing and see if there's anything else wrong with it."

"Great!" Potter exclaimed. "And while we're doing that, what will you be doing?"

Darius tried to hide his lack of enthusiasm as he replied. "I'll be calling Max."

II

"Have the FBI been put on the case?" Max asked when Darius had briefed him on the situation.

"I assume they will be," Darius replied, both relieved and surprised that Max was not being more confrontational.

"Well, I'll make sure they are. I want this person caught! Do you have any clues as to what he was after?"

"Who knows at this point? My people are certainly putting out some wild speculation, though. Potter seems to think they might have been looking to get access to the resonance feedback. Someone with inside information from Bionamic."

"Preposterous. I can't believe what I'm hearing! We take loyalty very seriously. Next you'll be saying that Doctor Young is somehow involved so you can demand to speak with him again. I don't have time for this, Darius. You see to it that we get the people responsible one way or the other."

The screen went blank as Max terminated the transmission. Darius shared a questioning glance with Igor and leaned back in his chair.

"For claiming to be so concerned, he's very reluctant to discuss it," Igor said.

"Yeah, he did act strangely, didn't he?"

Dave knocked on the door before they could discuss the matter further and poked his head in. "We've found something," he exclaimed.

III

Kim had been on edge all day, and now that the network analysis program had been discovered to have been left running—effectively overwriting the log of her transmission to Sue and the others—she was finding it hard to keep up the pretence of concerned ignorance. She had claimed to have no knowledge of why the program had been set to automatically restart, blaming it on the confusion of the morning's events. Dave, however, was not satisfied with this explanation and Kim was growing increasingly uneasy as he delved deeper into the intricacies of their system to try to find clues to what had happened.

It seemed inevitable that at some stage he would stumble across her authorisation codes, which in turn would expose the attempts she had made to obscure the transfer of the particles. As the afternoon wore on towards evening, she was feeling more and more agonised as she grew certain that she would be exposed at any minute. It was with a profound sense of relief that she saw Dave give up his attempts for the day and together with Potter turn his attentions toward their experiments with the resonance feedback. When she left at seven-thirty, having agreed to stay late along with the others, they were well into setting up the prototype.

When she arrived home to her apartment, all the pent-up tension was released and filled her with a feeling of despair. She ignored the blinking red light of the answering machine and poured herself a large glass of red wine, which she gulped down in a single continuous drink, then she shed her clothing and stepped into a hot shower. She needed to get a message off to Scott and the others, but she wanted to try to collect herself a little first, otherwise she didn't think she could put down what was happening without starting to cry.

After her shower, and pouring herself another glass of wine, Kim made an attempt at getting down the facts, without letting too much of her emotions shine through in the message. She knew, though, that there was no way to hide the uncertainty she felt about her future at Sytek and her ability to stay out of the hands of the FBI.

IV

If Kim was worrying about her fate, her compatriots were no less worried as they sat gathered around Sue's dinner table, having just listened to her read the message from Kim. Frank in particular was taking the news badly, the full responsibility for the situation resting, at least in the mind of Frank, firmly on his shoulders. Finley had never seen him so depressed.

"It's all my fault. We're all gonna be imprisoned and it'll be my fault. My children will have to grow up with their father in jail. What am I going to do?"

"Look," Finley said, trying to bring Frank out of his funk. "I was the one who couldn't get the computer out of there, and anyway, all of the things Kim's talking about, they haven't needed the clues from the computer to figure out. So nothing that's happened yet is really your fault."

"Right," Scott cut in. "In situations like this we just have to stay focused!"

"Focused, right. Focused, I see!" Frank scoffed. "You think the FBI are gonna give a shit about how focused we are, Scott? And the only reason the computer hasn't led them straight to us yet, is because Sytek doesn't have it. The feds will have access to it and they'll be coming straight here. I just know it!"

"Well, if we're lucky there won't be much of an investigation. You know how these high-profile companies want to avoid bad press at any cost," Finley said.

"Finley does have a point," Sue agreed. "Anyway," she added in a clumsy attempt at trying to cheer him up, "although I feel that you should have told us about the mess you made right away, there's no guarantee these transistors are going to lead them to your front door."

Frank sighed. "I know this, Sue. It doesn't make me worry less about it, though. I can't believe they went down there. What ever were they thinking?" Frank persisted. "I've managed to keep that cellar door locked for years, and the one time I don't is the one that's gonna get me put away," he went on, now nervously running his hand through his hair.

Scott slammed his hand down onto the table, almost upsetting Finley's glass of coke. "Nobody's going to jail!" he exclaimed. "There's only one thing we can do," Scott continued. "The rest of us will have to hit the road. Look, Frank, I feel responsible. I got you into this mess in the first place, it's only right I get you out of it. We'll go mobile for a while and you can tell the feds, assuming they ever show up at your front door, that I asked you to build the network computer."

"Now that sounds like an offer you can't refuse, Frank," Sue declared.

"It does, yeah. I'm not sure what to say, in fact," he agreed.

"How's about saying you'll do it," was Sue's response. "I'm not sure I like the sound of having to leave home, though. Are you sure the rest of us can't hole up at my place for a little? Just because the FBI get your name doesn't mean they'll know you and I have any connections, and it isn't like I don't have enough spare room."

"Nah, far too risky," Scott said. "We'll need to put some distance between us and the city, somewhere we can limit the potential of any interruptions. Out West perhaps; the middle-of-nowhere-Montana, maybe."

"You'd have no real technician, along," Frank remarked.

"That's right," Finley agreed, feeling the first stirrings of an objection to the plan. "Who's going to build me one of those prototype interfaces for this resonance feedback? I mean with all the secrecy surrounding that, it must be worth looking into it, right?"

"Intriguing stuff, for sure." Scott said. "But the main reason for all this was to help Sue get some information on her uncle's disappearance. We have our portal into Bionamic's system now, and if we're careful they won't be able to close it without getting hold of us or disentangling their whole network. That's the only thing that's bothering me, the only thing that could stop us now." Finley could see that Scott was trying to be grand about this, but the idea that they would have to leave this feedback effect unexplored was eating at him. He was about to protest when Sue came to his aid.

"As far as we know, my uncle was most probably investigating this very thing when he disappeared. Whatever it is, I would definitely like to know more," she said, looking thoughtful. "Anyway, Frank's been giving it some thought and it might be doable."

"The biggest problem is getting the right materials," he explained, seeming a bit more relaxed now; whether it was because of Scott's offer or because he wasn't at that moment thinking of the possibility of imminent capture by the FBI, Finley could not tell. "Most of the setup is like the kind of virtual reality glasses we've all seen at the techie-fairs. There would be one or two alterations, expensive changes mainly. Also, you'd need some specific machinery to make it come together as perfectly as possible." He shrugged. "We can't do much about that, but I think we can make something that's functionally similar, just not as sleek and pretty," Frank assertively added.

"So you think it can be done?" Finley asked.

"After what Scott has offered to do, I'd be willing to try to build you anything. But yeah, as a matter of fact, I think it can be done."

Sue clapped Frank's shoulder and grinned. "That's great. How is Maria, by the way? Is she in a more, relaxed state of mind at the present moment?"

"You're asking me?" Frank grunted. "I wouldn't know. Hardly spoken a word to me all last week." It sounded like he was complaining again, but it was the old type of complaining that they were used to, and Finley knew Frank was feeling more like himself already.

V

Dave watched with a growing sense of agitation as Tony helped Potter climb into the second-hand dentist's chair they had brought in to serve as a seat for the Resonance Explorer, as Potter wanted to call himself. After adjusting the prototype headset Bionamic had sent, Potter settled in. He was certain they had followed the instructions to the letter, but still, it was untested equipment. Untested prototype equipment. Anything could go wrong at this stage.

"You sure you want to go ahead with this?" Dave asked.

Potter nodded.

"Have we overlooked anything, Tony?" Dave called out to the younger man, who had moved over to the screens where the vital signs for Potter and the machinery were displayed side by side.

"Everything looks fine. Electro-magnetic readings seem to be at a minimum throughout the entire building. His heart rate is up a bit," Tony said, then muttered something more that Dave couldn't hear.

"What was that?" Dave asked.

"I said, 'Which isn't really all that surprising.'"

Dave nodded and turned back to Potter seated in the chair. "You still happy with five minutes? Are you sure that isn't—"

"I'll be fine," Potter interrupted. "What's all this worrying, Dave. I'm going to be fine."

"The slightest sign that anything's wrong and you're out of there."

"Fine, fine," came Potter's retort. "Just like we agreed. For heavens sakes, Dave, you're beginning to sound like Igor. You wanna sound like Igor for the rest of your life? or somebody with a bit of spunk."

"Good luck, Potter." Dave said humorously, wishing his buddy all the best, now heading for Tony and his place at the workstation. "Let's dispense with the countdown," he said. "You all set?" he then shouted down to Potter.

"Waiting your word," Potter called back. "Let's do this thing. Fire it up. I'll see both of you on the flipside."

After looking at each other in trepidation, and after watching Potter lower the visor over his head, Tony and Dave switched on the prototype's connection to the entanglement's resonance. Sitting next to Potter on the lab floor was the virtual visor's tall aluminium stand, connected to which was a long, flexible cable allowing the prototype to be repositioned to settle steadily onto Potter's face.

"Can you hear me?" Potter asked making some adjustment to a small microphone attached to the visor.

"Yes. You're coming through loud and clear," Tony replied.

"Good. The start-up sequence is going off in here. Interface active in ten seconds."

"That matches our numbers," Dave confirmed. "Now try to relax."

Potter gave a nervous giggle and replied, "You too, man."

"Right, here we go," Potter said as the countdown on the screens reached zero. "I can see the green clouds. They look similar to what we've been seeing on the screens, but they have, you know, three dimensions to them in here. Wow! I'm trying to...lines... Seems like..."

Dave looked over at Tony. "What happened?"

"I don't know. His vital signs haven't changed."

Potter's voice spoke up again, but this time in a disjointed, sluggish fashion. "Is there... What is that...?"

Dave gave Tony another worried look. "What's he talking about?"

"What can you see?" Tony asked, directing his question at Potter, but there was no response. "His theta cycles are on the move," Tony continued, pointing to the monitor.

"And there is a slight discrepancy in his EEG reading also," Dave agreed. "He's coming up to a minute. You think we should let him ride it out or what? Personally, I think we ought to get him out of there."

Considering the question for only a few seconds, Tony nodded in agreement. "You're right. If this thing is having an effect on his brain functions, I'd rather be safe than sorry."

Dave rapidly keyed in the command codes that would cut the connection to the resonance away from the visor. Potter's body relaxed visibly in the chair, making Dave realise with surprise just how tensed up he must have been before they broke the link.

They both ran over to Potter's side and removed the visor from his face, with Tony starting to disconnect him from the sensors. Dave patted first his arms and then his face in an effort to make him respond, but still it took him more than a minute to get Potter to focus on him, at which point he seemed to come abruptly to his full faculties.

"You back with us then?" Dave asked.

Potter removed the final sensors from his chest and leaped to his feet. "What happened?" he began. "I thought we agreed to five minutes!"

"Your readings were fluctuating in a way neither of us liked, so we had to bring you out early. I'm sorry."

"Early?" Potter looked at Dave as if he didn't understand what he was saying. "I must have been in there for at least fifteen minutes. I was afraid something had gone wrong, that or you'd forgotten about me."

Dave and Tony shared yet another worried look and Potter looked back and forth between them. "Are you serious?" he asked. "I wasn't in there for fifteen minutes?"

"Not even close," Dave said. "The connection was only active for one minute sixteen seconds. You can check the logs yourself."

Potter hurried over to the monitors to check the numbers while Tony stared at the visor as if he didn't recognise it. "What the hell is this thing?" he asked in a breathless whisper.

EIGHT

I

"Hey, Woodroe, looks to me like somebody's been trying to straighten up the living room," agent Mike O'Neill pointed out to his partner, agent Mark Woodroe, who had just entered from the garage. "Why's it only half-finished though?" he wondered aloud, standing in the hole in the floor where the cabling joined the room from the street.

"Bet that was somethin' to see. It's not everyday a Volvo comes crashing through a garage door," Woodroe remarked.

"What's that?" O'Neill asked, nodding at a glossy leaflet Woodroe had bagged and was carrying with him.

"Oh this," he replied holding the bag aloft.

"They, or someone, might have ordered out. Fallen down the side of the stove."

"That's another thing the police missed then," O'Neill grumbled clambering back onto the floorboards. "Call me old fashioned, but I don't think rearranging furniture is gonna be that high up on the list of priorities for somebody doing a job like this."

Woodroe nodded in agreement.

"Which leaves me asking the question, why that was the last thing he did before leaving? I mean who'd leave a job like this half finished?"

"Maybe he got bored?" Woodroe suggested.

"Not likely. More like interrupted," O'Neill said. "So what if we have several hackers in the process of getting themselves settled in and comfortable for a long wait. The furniture is being moved around to a formation that includes everyone when word comes through that their little party has been rumbled, and they don't want anyone to know just how many of 'em there are. Doing anything about that," O'Neill stared at the huge hole in the floor, "was never going to be that much of an issue. That'd account for why this place looks as it does."

"It also checks out with having someone on

the inside?"

"Right. Sytek, or the company running the cables for them. Who knows? Could be both for all we know. Assuming for one minute it was the only one guy acting alone, it's some coincidence that he'd be right in the middle of replacing all of this furniture when Sytek and the cable guys show up outside."

"Probably be packing up. 'Less he was in mid-hack," Woodroe agreed.

"Exactly. Why would he be moving furniture when he hasn't even pulled out all his cables? It's far more likely that there were several of them and they got a call telling them to blow. That little stunt with the car chase was planned to make us think there was only one person."

"So, next stop pizza?" Woodroe asked.

"Isn't it a bit early for lunch?" O'Neill joked.

"Never too early for pizza."

II

Darius's first contact with the FBI agents was over the phone.

"We figure it's better to call beforehand, Mr.

Daucourt," the agent introducing himself as O'Neill told him over a line that made him sound like a nasal game show host.

"That's fine. We'll be ready for you around twelve. Can I ask what exactly it is we should expect from your visit?"

"It's just a chat. Formalities mostly. We're checking all possible leads, you understand. Now, am I correct in saying there are eight of you working on this quantum internet?"

"That's correct."

"Sounds like exciting stuff, based on what I've been reading in the press. I look forward to seeing the place where it all happens. Anyway, Mr. Daucourt, we'll see you around lunchtime."

"I'll advise reception."

After hanging up the phone, Darius walked over to stand by the window looking out over the drum. Ray and Potter were deep in a discussion on theories explaining the time discrepancy Potter had experienced during their experiment with the feedback interface. That was yet another thing Darius felt was out of his control. He had been apprehensive of the outcome of their late-night experiment. Potter's story about floating in a featureless void, only vaguely aware of his physical surroundings and then something like a voice, was disturbing. It sounded like a bad dream—worse, it sounded like brain damage—but Potter insisted it was part of the phenomena and neither he nor Dave would let the matter go.

Kim was slipping out of his grasp as well, becoming more distant, reluctant to meet his eyes. *Is she worried that we will accuse her of being involved in the intrusion or is she worried that we will find out she is?* He felt a bit guilty about thinking it. It was true that Kim had reservations about Bionamic from the start, but could he honestly say that he hadn't thought those same thoughts, or at least very similar ones, before agreeing to take on the project?

That afternoon Darius found himself, along with Igor, across the table from the federal agents. The younger one, O'Neill, leaned forward and handed him a cardboard folder. "Do you recognise any of these people?"

"I didn't think you'd have any pictures of them so soon," Darius said, opening the folder.

"We don't have actual photographs, I'm afraid. These are sketches done from the descriptions and witness accounts of the rental office staff of the property and a local pizza place we have reason to believe they used. We're not even sure they were at the house, though it seems likely. I take it you don't recognise them?"

"I've never seen any of them before."

"I have to ask though, Mr. Daucourt," O'Neill continued, as Darius handed the images of two males and a female across to Igor.

"Car was stolen up in New York city," Woodroe said. "Might be a connection there. Still doesn't ring any bells?"

Darius shook his head, as did Igor, who handed the images back.

"Do you know if any of your employees have friends or relatives up there?" O'Neill continued.

Darius tried not to show his sense of unease. "I'm not sure I take your meaning."

"Your equipment specs aren't exactly public knowledge," Woodroe said.

"No, you're quite right. They aren't." Darius agreed. "And their information clearly came from somewhere, that much is evident. To answer your question, I don't really know."

"We're just a little unclear as to these hackers' motives. You wouldn't happen to know what those might be, would you?"

O'Neill stated more than asked, staring at him with an unchanging expression. Had he been anyone else, Darius would have stood up and walked out.

"So you think I'm holding something back, and you're telling me to play ball. Okay. What am I supposed to do to show my good faith? Point out my least favourite employee or the person I think is the least trustworthy?" Darius didn't really know why he was feeling offended. The FBI's approach did make sense from their point of view, even if he would have preferred to deal with any wrongdoing in-house, as it were. These were his people.

"We're not out to find a scapegoat here. Simply put, we'd like to rule out the potential for any bribery right off the bat," O'Neill said, relenting in his stare and relaxing his stance a bit. "Can you be certain that nobody here has any involvement with what's happened?" When Darius didn't reply, the agent continued, "I gather you haven't received any demands?"

"No, no demands."

"And you haven't noticed anything unusual? Even the smallest detail may be helpful."

"No, nothing unusual," Darius said. O'Neill's frown was telling him the agent had been expecting to hear something different. O'Neill turned to Woodroe who reached back into his attaché case bringing out another picture.

"Ever seen this man before?" Woodroe asked, sliding an out-of-focus black and white still-shot across the desk.

"Is this the driver?" Darius asked.

"Recognise him?"

"I'm afraid not. It'd be difficult from that angle at the best of times."

"We only got a quick glance at him, agent Woodroe," Igor added as Darius passed him the photograph. "Did this come from the mall? I don't think he was wearing a cap when we saw him."

O'Neill nodded in what Darius thought seemed to be a resigned way and when Igor handed the picture back to Woodroe the agent put it away keeping it separate from the other images. "Any idea what that is he's carrying?" Woodroe asked.

"Sorry. Presumably part of the equipment he used. I really wish we could be more helpful," Darius offered.

O'Neill nodded again, his demeanour changing. "Unless forensics find something on the car, or they've made some headway with the computer that our friend left in it, there's not a lot of concrete information to go on. If we could establish a credible motive, that would at least be a start. Taking on high-profile targets like Sytek or Bionamic requires serious motivation. Do you know anything about your UK partners that might be useful to the investigation?"

"Bionamic," Woodroe said, surprising Darius with the note of disdain in his voice.

Darius resisted the urge to look at Igor. "I appreciate your position, agent O'Neill, but as I've already told you, we are equally at a loss here. Our relationship with Bionamic is strictly business. We don't have any insight into their inner workings."

"And as for possible motives," Igor began, "we don't work in an area that has a lot of competition, certainly not the sort of area likely to encourage this level of corporate espionage."

"Yeah, that does match the impression we got. I've been reading up on your progress. In fact, I read a few articles even before I knew about the case," O'Neill said. "I wasn't quite expecting to have any direct involvement with any of this....... Quantum Entanglement." He looked out the window at the machines covering the lab floor. "Very exotic! The papers really don't explain it in any great detail, though."

"Well, it's always hard to condense masses of science into a catchy article. Especially if you don't know what you are talking about. I could tell you about some of the general theory if you like, but if you want details about the research, again about the best I could do would be to direct you to Bionamic."

"Somehow I don't think we're going to get much information from there." O'Neill said, turning to look at his partner with a wry smile.

"The fact is, agent O'Neill, we're working on a very specific contract with Bionamic. We don't conduct any of our own research on the quantum internet because any of its future spin-off technologies are more financially advantageous to us if we haven't registered the patent." Darius made his point that he had nothing to hide rather well. "Except for being allowed to play with some cutting-edge technology, we're little more than a glorified ISP."

There was a short silence where O'Neill seemed to be considering further questions, before he gathered up the images he had been showing them earlier into a pile and nodded.

"Right. Well, we need to interview your employees now. Can we continue to use this room?"

III

Darius was in the drum keeping himself distracted from the interviews being conducted by the FBI when Igor walked up to him, eyeing the corridor leading to the conference room. "Potter should be done soon," he said.

Darius followed his gaze and nodded even though he hadn't really been keeping track. He had only caught sight of the interviewees now and then as one or the other left to use the washroom, or grab a coffee.

"They resent this, you know," Igor continued, lowering his voice. "None of them were expecting to be questioned by the FBI. Has anybody in your family, or social group, expressed more than a passing interest in your work? What kind of question is that?"

"The kind you ask when you're working for the FBI," Darius told him. "You know what they're up to. It's not so much what you say as how you say it."

"Still, it's going a bit too far, don't you think?"

"We don't have the luxury of knowing everything they do," Darius continued as Potter rejoined the others looking decidedly flustered.

"Another satisfied customer," Igor sneered, before quickly turning back to Darius with a curious look on his face. "What do you mean, we don't know what they know?"

"We don't know their agenda. Since Max was the one calling them in, he's the one aiming them."

"You're saying Max is leaning on the FBI to find the problem in our camp?" Igor asked.

"Maybe not us specifically, but I bet the first thing Max would have done is try to exonerate Bionamic from having anything to do with any of this. I also think there'll be pressure put on these feds to find a problem anywhere but at Bionamic, which makes it all the more important that Kim's little network blunder remains '*sub-sigillo*'. Just like any mention of the feedback research."

Igor was quite for a moment. "What exactly are you saying?"

"Well what if the feds have been told to

seize anything that can be connected to the work we do with Bionamic? Max seemed very eager to find out what Potter and Dave have been up to."

"Her blunder being the opportunity they need to start digging around, you mean? I should be more surprised!" Igor paused to consider the point, then added. "I didn't think it would be this uncomfortable," he paused again. "What if she did have something to do with it? Not mentioning it might backfire on us, if they figure it out themselves. Did Dave ever work out what actually happened?"

"No. Not yet. He got side tracked with other things," Darius replied, looking across at the others spread out at their desks. "I suppose the real question we ought to be asking ourselves is whether or not she's just recognised any of those people?" O'Neill and Woodroe stood up in the conference room and made their way to the door.

"So, how are we playing this?" Igor asked.

"Up front and in their faces. See if we can't put them on the spot, even things up a little. With any luck, they'll let something slip or we'll be able to tell if either of them are holding anything back." Darius left for his office.

"So how went it? Am I allowed to ask?" Darius queried the agents.

"Officially, we're not supposed to say," Woodroe replied.

"But, unofficially, you'll no doubt be pleased to hear we've got no reason to believe anybody withheld anything from us," O'Neill continued.

"So my people are off the hook?"

"We of course can't rule anything out at the moment."

"Not even Bionamic being the source of the leak?" Darius returned O'Neill's earlier dispassionate stare with as much intensity as he could.

"You have reason to think they're involved?"

"Nothing other than that they probably have a lot more enemies than Sytek does. And probably a lot more disgruntled employees. There are all kinds of rumours about them flying around."

"Like what?" O'Neill asked, raising his eyebrows a fraction.

"Have you ever heard about Professor Melvin Young?"

"Ah. The disappearance. Yes, we have, we've been in contact with New Scotland Yard."

"Any truth to it?"

"Professor Young was reported missing and there were accusations of kidnapping made. As far as we know, though, there was never a formal hearing."

"Do you think it might be related?"

"I can assure you we investigate all possibilities, however unlikely. Even the online rumours about Sytek."

Darius frowned. "What kind of rumours?"

"Mainly about the type of work it is you're involved with, and whether it's really safe. Along with some more crazy theories about where you or Bionamic got the technology from. It seems some people were suspicious of your altruistic mission statement even before this project, pointing to your liaison with Bionamic as proof that you aren't as benign as you pretend to be." O'Neill held up his hands in a warding gesture. "I know, you've already explained that you don't do any actual research, but that doesn't change the fact that some people out there might think you are more involved than you claim. Perhaps one of these people targeted you or one of your employees with misinformation or some sort of scam to get the information they needed. We're not saying that one of your people has gone bad, but how do you know they haven't been fooled into thinking they're doing the right thing?"

Woodroe leaned forward in his seat. "How about it? Have any do-good crusaders in your group?"

Darius looked away, sharing a brief worried look with Igor.

* * *

"Did I imagine it or did Kim Knowles linger with the sketches?" O'Neill asked later when the agents were sitting in their car.

"She held onto them alright," Woodroe agreed. "Might have just found our first solid lead with that one."

O'Neill turned his notebook to the page detailing what they knew about Kim. "She's worked at Sytek for a little over two years. Moved up from California but she grew up here in DC. Ah, this is more like it. She went to college in New York, where it seems a cross reference search with her name and Bionamic lands a match. Looks like she signed an online petition against them whilst she was there. Get that!" He tossed his notebook onto the dashboard and started the car's engine.

As O'Neill reversed out of the parking space, Woodroe uploaded their recorded interviews to his tablet PC. "Didja see the look Daucourt and his partner exchanged at the end?" Woodroe mused. "If they haven't considered her before, they probably will now."

"I'm more intrigued about them mentioning Young. Which one of the group do you think might have told them about that?"

"Maybe he'd have let something slip if you'd kept talking."

"Maybe, but at the moment keeping him in the dark is gonna be our best policy. It wouldn't have served any useful purpose to tell him that the investigators working the kidnapping case over in England thought that their efforts were being sabotaged. That would only have given him ammunition to try to divert suspicion from himself and his colleagues."

"Yeah. Still strange though. The whole thing about Young is unexpected."

"Yeah. It sure is," O'Neill agreed, fingers drumming on the steering wheel.

NINE

"Are we testing all of these filters?" Sue asked.

Frank turned away from his screen. Having been deeply engrossed in his work, calibrating their IPAS settings according to the instructions they had received from Kim, he had almost forgotten that he wasn't alone in his basement workshop.

"Yeah, I suppose we'd better, just to be on the safe side. Hey, you fancy taking a breather?" Frank asked. "I could definitely do with a sandwich of some description."

He stood up to go ask Maria if she would make them lunch, but froze when he caught a glimpse of the driveway-cam monitor, a sinking sensation filling his gut. "I didn't think they'd get here this quick."

"What?" Sue asked behind him.

"Company!" Frank exclaimed, before making a high-speed sprint to the staircase, calling out for Maria in a hushed frenzy. He looked back at Sue, before disappearing up the stairs, leaving her alternating between glancing worriedly at the empty doorframe and the monitor showing their unwelcome visitors at the front of the house.

Frank opened the door to the hallway upstairs as the doorbell rang, managing to catch hold of Maria's arm as she passed by on her way to see who was calling. "Tell them I'm not in."

She looked confused, then suspicion filled her eyes. "You lousy bastard. Frank Moretto, you lousy bastard," Maria hissed at him.

"Shhh! Please, not now. Maria, just get rid of them, alright. Just do it, will you please?" He glanced down the stairs to see Sue at the bottom step, listening to what was happening above. "Come on already, help me move this damn coat stand in front of the door!" He added.

Maria half-heartedly lent in against the coat stand glaring at him throughout. "What exactly is it you're up to down there?" She asked. "If you've brought trouble here—"

"Tell them I'm fishing. Come on Maria!" Frank insisted, and the large piece of furniture slid into position across the doorframe. Frank half closed the door to the basement and turned off the lights before backing down the stairs, almost losing his footing when the doorbell rang again.

He could feel Sue settling down next to him on the lower step as Maria opened the front door in the hallway outside.

"Morning!" She could be heard to say answered by a warm, but professional sounding voice. "Good morning, Ma'am. I'm agent O'Neill with the FBI."

"Really. Sure you've got the right address?" Maria asked tersely.

"Do you mind if we come in, Ma'am?"

"Well, as a matter of fact, I do. It's not that I'd object, normally, but you've caught me on the hop, so to speak. I haven't got a lot of time, agent... I'm just in the middle of getting ready for an appointment, you see," Maria said. "And then I'm spending a few days with my mother."

Frank slowly let out the breath he had been holding in and rested his head against the wall. The line about going to her mother's place was obviously for his benefit, but at least she was covering for him.

"Your husband home?" another, deeper voice asked. Frank assumed it belonged to the other agent.

"My husband, Frank. Is it him you're here to see. He hasn't…"

"We just need to ask him a few questions, that's all," the first agent continued. "Where is he, Maria?"

"He's fishing. Left early this morning."

"I see. And do you expect him back anytime soon?"

Frank could hear the sarcasm in Maria's responding laugh. "That's a good question. Let me think. The last time he disappeared, fishing, it was only for a few days. The time before that, he was gone for nearly a week. I assume he'll give me a call when he's decided how much he's enjoying himself. Is there anything else I can do for you?"

"Does he have a cell phone with him?"

"He does, but it wont be on. He'll only switch it on when he wants to make a call. Wait here a sec. I'll get you his number and you can try calling him for yourself."

Frank crept down the stairs as quickly as possible to the table where he had left his phone, trying to avoid the noisy step. He fumbled over the table in the poor light until he found it and shut it off. When he returned to the stairs, he could hear that the conversation had moved on.

"When you do hear from him, let him know we want to talk to him. Here's my card," O'Neill's voice said.

"Soon," the other man added.

The front door closed and Frank waited a few moments before turning on the lights in the basement again. Sue made her way down the steps to watch the agents leave on the monitor.

"Thank you, Maria," Frank called through the door. On the other side, the coat rack was pulled over and the basement door slammed open to reveal a furious Maria.

"You're a fool, Moretto. You've really landed in the shit this time. The FBI?" she screamed. "Well, I'm not gonna stick around just to save your sorry ass. I'm leaving, I'm taking the children with me and I'm leaving. You can figure this one out by yourself."

When Maria had stopped slamming doors, Frank rejoined Sue in the basement.

"Are you okay?" she asked, looking down at

her hands. "Why didn't you talk to them? Did you forget Scott's plan?"

He shrugged, blushing slightly. He had forgotten all about the plan in the initial panic, and once he had remembered, it felt like it was too late. "I forgot. I don't know. Can't explain that one. Come on, we don't even have the IPAS finished, yet. You can't take it on the road in its current state. And what if those agents had asked to take a look around the house? You'd be caught up in this as well."

"Then you'd have asked to see a search warrant. But, no, you're right," Sue conceded. "That might have raised more suspicion and have them calling in surveillance."

"You think they'll do that?" Frank asked. He hadn't thought about that. If Maria found out that he had done something to cause the FBI to put their home under surveillance, she might never come back.

"No, I think they need to have more probable cause for that sort of thing. But they *will* be back and your fishing story has complicated things no end."

"Yeah. I guess they will."

"I don't mean in a few days, Frank. I mean later today. If they tracked you down through that transistor, then it's likely they are parked somewhere in the neighbourhood, waiting for their search warrant to come through from some friendly judge."

"Shit, seriously, you think? You think they'll bother Maria again when she leaves for her mothers?" He looked up at the ceiling, where Maria was presumably packing her things above them. Sue prodded him in the chest and he looked back at her face.

"Maria will be fine. They might stop her car to make sure she isn't helping you escape, assuming they didn't buy that fishing trip story at face value, but other than that I don't think they'll mind her leaving. It's easier to search an empty house."

"So what do we do?" Frank asked dejectedly. "What was the point of having Maria lie for me if they're just going to find us both here in a few more minutes?"

"Calm down, Frank. We're not giving up, but we do have to get out of here, somehow. Pack up all of this gear and whatever you think you might need for a few days. Don't leave anything incriminating lying around either. Oh, and don't forget your fishing stuff."

Frank nodded. "What will you be doing?"

"I'm going to call Scott. He'll have to come pick us up."

"Here, outside in the street, what if those feds see him?"

"No not here, in the street. If we use the back door and head away from the front, can we reach some likely pick-up point within the next hour or so?"

"I guess if we cut across some lawns we could reach the old timber line running alongside parkway. We could be there in half an hour."

She nodded and pulled up Scott's number on her cell phone.

The next hour went by in focused activity for Frank. He found that the only way he could deal with the fact that Maria was leaving with the children—again—was to try not to think about it. She'd gone off to stay with her mother before, but she'd always come back. She'd be back this time too. Wouldn't she?

They managed to pack everything up faster than he thought they would. Sue convinced him to suppress his OCD-urge to go over everything in the house three times in case he missed something that would connect him to some other hack he had done in the past. They made their way out the back and across next door's yard, apparently unseen. Once Scott picked them up, they brought everything to Sue's place where they dropped her off along with the IPAS and a promise that Finley would be over to help her do the final calibrations. During the ride, they had decided the only way to make the fishing story stick was to have someone to corroborate it. Scott broke a few speed limits to get Frank up to Lake Zoar in time for him to pretend he had just stepped off the bus. Frank called up several of his friends on the way to the lake, finally managing to persuade one of them to "join him" there.

When Finley arrived at Sue's house, she had just finished the first phase of tests on the IPAS and he was immediately put to work double-checking what she had done.

"There's a present for you in the bag in the hall," he told her when she served him a glass of iced tea.

Sue raised an eyebrow. "What kind of present?" she asked.

"I guess it's for all of us really," Finley explained. "It's the prototype interface Scott and I have been working on. We've almost got it together the way we think it's supposed to be, but neither of us have the degrees around here. I thought maybe you could look it over and maybe we could take it for a spin later."

"It's not a sports car, Fin," she said dismissively, but she did fetch the bag and emptied its contents onto the other side of the table, sitting down to look through it all. "Where's the print out Frank gave you? The one with the list of specifications?" she asked.

"Oh. Yeah, in my jacket," he said, gesturing towards the hall only to remember that his jacket was in fact hanging on the back of the chair he was sitting on. "Here, they here." He gave Sue a grin and reached into his inside pocket to retrieve the folded sheets of paper.

Finley waited as Sue went through the settings, occasionally looking over at her, laughing to himself at the way she tutted when she found something he had connected in the wrong way. When she got to the end of the list, she went back over them in the opposite direction, trying to find anything they might have missed.

"Well, is there anything wrong with it?" Finley asked. "Please tell me it's now time to run the diagnostics."

"Mmm," was the reply from Sue, who was

comparing the insides of the visor she was holding to the diagram in the instructions. Finley smiled again and started the diagnostics tool anyway, rows of text travelling up the screen informing him that things were as they should be. As had happened in the house where they had first accessed Sytek's network, green dots started to fill in the window labelled Resonance Feedback. At first he managed to concentrate on the numbers listed, comparing them to the expected output, but he soon found that his gaze was repeatedly drawn to the dots amassing into patterns in the lower left corner of the screen, and when the diagnostic was complete and all the dots were in place, dancing to their unseen musician, Finley found himself captivated by their movement.

"What do you mean?" Sue said, making him look up.

"Uhm... What?" he said, blinking his eyes, finding that they were itchy and dry.

"What you just said."

"I didn't say anything," he countered, wondering if he had. He had wanted to say something, he remembered that much.

"Yes, you did. You said something about space, then you asked me who I was." Sue examined him carefully. "Are you on something? Because if you are, I should check those figures myself."

Finley tried to give her a confident smile. "I don't do drugs. You know that, they space me out too much." Sue seemed unable to suppress a giggle at this. "Anyway, I wasn't talking to you..." This realization made him stop in his tracks. *So who was I talking to,* Finley wondered, the ever-changing green shapes on the screen doing their best to recapture his attention, but he willed himself not to look and turned off the diagnostics. "I think everything is in order here. How are you coming along?" he asked.

Sue held up the modified visor proudly. "Straightening out your mistakes wasn't so bad, it should work pretty well, maybe as well as the original, but don't quote me on that. Provided the original ever worked, of course." She shrugged. "I don't know who designed the thing and I'm not a brain-surgeon, but I do question what possible purpose stimulating those areas of the brain could have."

Finley stretched his hand out, trying not to show how eager he was. "I'll give it a go if you like," he said. She looked at him, weighing the newly created interface in her hand as if it would help her tell whether it was safe or not.

"Alright," she said finally, handing the device across to him. "I'll make a coffee."

Finley looked at the device now in his hands. It was ugly as hell and he suspected that he would look ridiculous wearing it, but he didn't care. What was giving him pause was the feeling that something momentous was about to happen. With a few taps of the keyboard the interface program Kim had provided was restarted. Then he settled the device over his eyes and ears and leaned back in his chair. There was a countdown, both on the displays in front of him and by a computer-generated voice in his ears. Then he found himself enveloped by green clouds.

TEN

I

Sue took one last look at her home before getting into the SUV where Scott was waiting. In retrospect Frank's fishing story had been a godsend, helping to focus their minds on the road trip. She'd never been on the run from the authorities before and didn't have a list of dos and don'ts handy. In fact, she'd never been on the run at all before, except for that one time when she ran away from home as a child. She had spent two hours in a nearby wood until she was cold and tired, and she then returned home to find that her mother had thought she'd been playing in her room the whole time.

Reluctantly, Sue got into the car, followed

by Finley who jogged up from the house, where he had been on his knees in the flowerbed.

"Is it secure? It's in a safe place I take it!" she asked as he took his seat in the back.

"Yeah. Like you told me: green plastic bag in one of the bushes. It's pointing right at the front door."

"You put up a hidden camera, Sue?" Scott asked.

"A little advance warning won't do us any harm," she replied. "It's hooked up to a motion sensor and we'll receive the captured footage of anyone going up to the door via email."

Scott nodded, pulling the SUV out into the street and setting them on their course toward the highway. "Is there any specific reason you want that many pictures of your mailman?" he asked. Finley tittered in the backseat.

"I just... think we need to know if the feds come by. If nothing else, it'll tell us when to stop using our cell phones." There was more to it, but she found it hard to explain to Scott. She felt vulnerable leaving her home, being where she couldn't defend it or protect her possessions. This way, even though she still couldn't do anything, she would at least know if anyone gained access while she was away.

"So did you get everything up and running?" Scott asked, letting the subject of the camera go.

"Hell yeah," Finley replied. "The magic gate is purring like finely tuned clockwork and the goggles of wonderment are tricked out to spec."

"You're speaking out loud now, Fin, not talking to yourself in your head," Sue said, turning to Scott to explain. "What Finley actually means is that the IPAS is calibrated correctly as far as we can tell and we even managed to put it together with the interface device."

"Really? That is nice, Sue."

"You and Finley did all the hard work. It went smoother than expected really. We..." She looked over her shoulder at Finley who only smiled at her in return. "We even had time to test the goggles."

Scott turned to look at her, flickering his eyes back and forth between her and the road. "So... what happened?"

"Watch the road, Scott!" Sue snapped, noticing the car was drifting hazardously close to the verge.

"Sorry, sorry," Scott said, righting the wheel.

Sue could feel the tension of the unanswered question all the way to the freeway, but Scott didn't ask again and Finley didn't volunteer an answer.

"I really don't know what happened," Sue said finally, deciding to break the silence. "When I tried the device there was mostly just a green haze all around me that looked more like cloud after a while. At first they just looked like individual dots grouped together, then the cloudscape began to appear. You kind of forgot you were sitting in a chair at home. It really felt like you were floating in the middle of nowhere, surrounded by these odd green swirling clouds."

"That's unbelievable!" Scott exclaimed. Sue hesitated, wondering if she should continue. She looked back at Finley who shrugged at her even though he hadn't turned away from looking out of the side window.

"What?" Scott asked. "What aren't you telling me?"

"Finley says he saw my uncle," she had to say it, voice low, still looking back at the rear seat. Finley's eyes snapped forward, giving her a pointed look, then he turned away and sighed, his shoulders sagging.

"That isn't exactly what I said. I wish I hadn't told you now."

Sue turned around in her seat, facing forwards. "I know."

Scott thumped the steering wheel in frustration. "Will one of you please just tell me what he did see then?"

Sue could hear Finley draw a breath and she felt guilty for starting up their argument from the night before.

"Some sort of structure," he finally explained. "It really is some sort of three dimensional space, like virtual reality. It was all very fuzzy, very indistinct, at first—just like Sue said—but after a bit I got the impression I was inside some kind of structure."

"And?" Sue said, finding herself unable to refrain from pushing him on.

"And I think I saw some people. Well, figures; fuzzy areas of density within the cloud." Sue turned to look at him and found him staring defiantly back. "And one of them kind of, sort of—"

"Looked like my uncle," Sue finished for him.

"Like the picture of your uncle from the newspaper you showed us," Finley countered. "The tiny, blurry, badly lit shot of your uncle turned into a black and white rasterized image

180

for a newspaper. There was no way to tell if it really looked like him. I could hardly make out any features and I only saw them for a few seconds before they all dissolved again in amongst all that green static."

Sue almost growled at him. He had seemed so sure when he had taken off the interface device and now he was denying it. It frustrated her to no end. She had spent what felt like hours last night trying to see the things that Finley had said he'd seen, but for her there was nothing but green clouds. "But you said—"

Scott placed a hand on her shoulder, still watching the road intently. "If Finley says he can't be sure, then he isn't sure. Whatever he said yesterday was said in the heat of the moment, right?"

"Right," she agreed. "But—"

"Now think back to other things Finley has said."

Sue was about to argue again, but then she did as Scott suggested. She remembered Finley telling her that her mailman looked like Mr. Magoo and wondering if he would deliver a note to Bugs Bunny. Finley arguing that there was no way to know for certain that gravity was a constant force, since it could be acting up

181

"when no one is looking." Finley deciding to eat breakfast in alphabetical order, just to see if it was tastier that way. And she started to giggle. "I'm sorry, Fin," she said, trying not to burst into laughter as Scott gave her a grin. Then she failed and Scott joined her. She grinned back at Finley who just looked back and forth between them.

"Apology accepted," he said. "Now have Scott pay attention to where we are going. Last time he laughed this much while driving, he missed an exit and we ended up in Atlantic City."

"Well," Scott said, calming down a little. "It's easy to laugh around you, Finley. It's one of the great things about you."

"One of many," Finley replied confidently.

II

As dusk fell, the truck containing Frank and Chris—Frank's last-minute fishing buddy—pulled to a halt outside Frank's house. Chris turned off the motor and Frank stopped staring out into the darkness, straining to see whether there was a dark car parked anywhere nearby.

"You alright, Frank?" Chris asked. "You look like you're on edge."

Frank smiled self-consciously. "Sorry, yeah, a little. I haven't really been good company have I?"

Chris smiled. "You've been fine, man. When you've been able to take your mind off whatever it is that's bugging you. You sure you don't want to talk about this?"

Frank looked out through the windshield again, then let out a loud sigh, deciding it would be better to tell his friend half the truth. "It's just... Before I left for the lake I had a row with Maria. One of those big ones, you know, with threats of leaving and all that. It's been on my mind all through the trip. That's why I've been having trouble relaxing. And now I don't see her car on the drive, you know."

Chris peered out into the darkness, unconsciously copying the look Frank had sported only seconds before. Then he smiled again. "I'm sorry to hear that, man, but don't worry too much. Maria loves you, otherwise she wouldn't be turning me down all the time."

Frank raised an eyebrow. "Don't go there, Chris," he warned, but a smile was playing at the corner of his lips.

"What? She's only human. What woman could resist all this?" He indicated his own portly frame with a sweeping gesture. "I'm telling you, if she prefers you over me, then she must be in love."

"You bastard," Frank laughed. "You never did have any sense of propriety."

"A what now?" Chris asked mock-flinching when Frank punched him on the shoulder. "Seriously though, Frank," he continued. "She'll be back. She's always come back in the past, right?"

"Right," Frank said, without any real conviction. "Thanks for the company, man. I had a good time. All things considered." He opened the door and jumped down from the cab.

"Anytime, Frank," Chris called out to him.

Frank clambered onto one of the rear wheels and hauled his fishing gear from the pickup's bed along with the one fish he had managed to catch. When he was back on the ground, he walked around to the side door, slamming it shut. Chris started the truck and waved at him as he pulled away from the house. As he drove off, the rumbling V8 engine echoed through the mostly empty residential street.

Dragging himself to his front door, Frank tried desperately not to look around like a paranoid criminal. Inside, his house was in darkness and he turned on the lights before carrying his fish through to the kitchen, leaving the rest of his stuff in the hallway. Running a sink of cold water Frank splashed some on his face and towelled himself off. He really wanted a shower, but he was half-expecting to be interrupted by the FBI at any minute, so he sat down at the kitchen table, staring at the plastic bag containing the dead fish. If anyone was watching him, he'd probably be a sorry sight. The thought brought him back to what Scott had said when he dropped him off at the lake. *Remember to act normal when you get back to the house. Do the things you would normally do. Remember, you've just been on a fishing trip. You've done that hundreds of times before.*

So what would he normally do? He looked down at his dirty hands, which reminded him of his first impulse when he came home. *Right. A shower then.*

* * *

He had time to get a shower and get dressed before he heard three loud knocks on the door. Putting the knife he had planned to use to gut the fish back in the drawer, he wandered into the hallway and flicked the outside light on, peering at the figures on the porch through the narrow stained-glass window in the door.

"Open the door, please. FBI," one of the men called out.

Taking a quick glance to confirm his coat stand was in the correct position, and fumbling for his glasses, Frank opened the door.

"Frank Moretto?" The smaller man asked.

"Yes." Straightening his spectacles was more of a nervous thing.

"I'm Agent O'Neill, this is agent Woodroe. We're from the FBI," the smaller man announced, holding his badge forward. "Probably be best if we have this discussion off the street, can we come in?"

Frank stepped to the side and the agents walked in.

"Been on a trip?" the agent called Woodroe asked, eyeing the fishing equipment on the hall floor.

"Yeah, I have. I got back about half an hour ago. Just what exactly is it I can do for you two gentlemen?"

"You alone, Frank?"

"So it would appear," Frank said. He made his way back into the kitchen, with the agents in tow and cleared the fish off the table, setting it down on the kitchen counter. When he put it down, he noticed his hands were trembling and clenched his fists to make them stop. "I was just going to make some coffee and clean my supper. Do you want a cup?"

"Where is Mrs. Moretto?" O'Neill asked.

"Her mother's. She doesn't like sleeping in the house on her own, with only the children. I can't say as I blame her, really."

"Trouble at the homestead?" asked O'Neill. "We spoke with your wife the day you left. She seemed upset."

"Is that right? Well seeing as arguing with your wife isn't a federal crime, I'd prefer not to discuss it with you," Frank replied, reaching over to turn on the coffee machine. "Did you want some coffee, or are you not planning to stay very long?"

"I'll pass," Woodroe said.

"None for me either, thanks," O'Neill added.

"Well in that case, I think it's about time you explained yourselves. Presumably you didn't come over just to hang out in my kitchen, and I'm pretty sure I got my tax returns in on time last year."

"Not our job anyway," Woodroe stated coldly.

"So what is it you want then? How can I be of service."

"We'd just like to ask you some questions," O'Neill said.

Frank turned the coffee maker off again and sat down, gesturing for the agents to do the same. "Ask away. Let's get this over with."

"Okay. Why don't we start with the easy ones, like where you've just come from?"

"Like I said, I've been fishing. What has that got to do with anything?" Frank objected. "Am I suspected of fishing without a licence now? Cause I didn't think that was your job either."

"Just answer the question, Mr. Moretto. Unless, that is, you'd prefer to finish the rest of our conversation at a local police station."

Frank deflated a little in his chair. "You know where I've come from. I've been on a fishing trip. Up north at Lake Zoar."

"Is there anyone who can corroborate that? Or did you go up there alone?"

"I went up alone—it was a spur of the

moment thing. I called a few friends on my way up there, but most of them were busy. Finally got hold of an old buddy who joined me up there."

"Buddy have a name?" Woodroe asked.

"Chris. Chris Sawyer."

"Chris got an address? Phone?" Woodroe continued.

"Sure he has, and I'll be happy to tell you it just as soon as you let me know what this is really all about."

O'Neill seemed to be studying him, then nodded and retrieved a small transistor from a zipped pocket. "Ever seen this before, Frank?" he asked, holding the tiny blue oval up to the light, and placing it in the centre of the kitchen table.

Trying to maintain his composure, Frank nodded. "I've seen thousands. There must be ten billion transistors like that in circulation."

"Not *just* like this one, Frank," Woodroe said.

"This one came out of a special computer," O'Neill explained. "A computer connected to a crime. This little transistor has a quite unique function within that computer, and that uniqueness makes it traceable, Frank. And we traced its purchase back to you."

Frank swallowed deeply. "I thought that might be it," he said, launching into the story he and Scott had put together. "A friend of mine asked me to put something together for him but he wouldn't tell me what it was for. Just gave me the specs and told me to follow them."

"Friend's name?"

Frank glanced at Woodroe, but directed the answer to O'Neill. "I wouldn't want to get him into any trouble."

"Your friend is already in trouble, Mr. Moretto. Unless you want to be in considerably more trouble, you will give us the name."

"Scott," Frank said after a brief pause. "Scott Guest."

"So this Mr. Guest, your friend, turns up at your door with some blueprints asking you to build a computer, no questions asked, and you don't think that's just a little strange, Frank?" O'Neill asked.

Frank hung his head. The laugh was half-hearted, more personal. "When you put it like that, it doesn't sound so great."

"How much did you charge him, Frank? I presume you didn't work for nothing. Is this gonna turn into an IRS issue after all?"

"I've known Scott for years," Frank protested.

"So you are friends then?"

"I guess, no. Well, sort of—I don't know."

"Frank, we're asking you the easy questions, here. You don't know if you are friends or not?"

"Yeah, I guess we're friends. At least I've known him for a long time. I only charged him the price of the parts and he gave me a case of beer for the work. I don't see him a lot. He comes around now and then when he needs help with his computer or something."

"And how often would that be?"

"I don't know. Once a month, maybe?"

"Lot of help with a PC," Woodroe stated and O'Neill nodded.

"I agree. I have a PC at home and I don't have that much trouble with it."

"So he comes around here for a chat. Am I going to get into trouble for any of this?" Frank asked.

"Not right now. But I hope you haven't got any more fishing trips planned."

Frank shook his head. "I don't."

"Good, because leaving town would not be in your best interests."

The agents stood up and marched out into the hall.

They paused by the front door. "If there is anything you'd like to add to your story, anything you might have...forgotten, here's where you contact me." O'Neill handed Frank his card. "Now you were about to give us numbers and addresses for your friends Chris Sawyer and Scott Guest."

Frank took a pad and a pen from the hallway table and jotted the information down on it.

"Do you and this Mr. Guest have any mutual friends?" O'Neill asked.

Frank shook his head.

"Is that a no, Frank?"

"Yeah. I mean, no, none that I can think of."

Woodroe gazed at Frank in silence, before suddenly starting to smile. "If you're lying to us, you will regret it."

Frank nodded.

"Right, well we won't keep you any longer," O'Neill said, opening the door to let himself and his colleague out.

Frank closed his front door feeling drained. Turning, he looked back to the hall table where he'd noticed an envelope with his name on it, leaning up against Maria's Chinese vase.

III

Agents Woodroe and O'Neill returned to their car where Woodroe used his laptop to bring up Chris and Scott's details to confirm their addresses and telephone numbers. O'Neill asked him to check if either of them had a record.

"Nothing on the fisherman," Woodroe said. "Something on Guest though. Check this out." He pointed at the screen and O'Neill leaned in to take a closer look.

"Hacking into, where?" O'Neill began.

"Arrested on suspicion of hacking into the school computers in college. This raises many questions. Like why he would need any help with his computers for one. There's more," Woodroe continued, again pointing to the appropriate line on the screen.

"Kim Knowles!" O'Neill couldn't hide his surprise. "Well what'ah ya know. Funny, her name showing up on his police report."

"Just a mention during the questioning. So, what next?" Woodroe asked.

"Next we go have ourselves a talk with this Mr. Scott Guest," O'Neill said, starting the car and pulling out into the road.

ELEVEN

I

"I saw you all when you arrived first thing," Mrs. Russo explained in her broad New York accent as she invited O'Neill and Woodroe into her apartment. "I had no idea you'd be coming here though, so I went to the grocery store. I found your card when I got home. So that's when I decided to call you, when I saw the card." She showed the agents into a small living room with an oversized television and red leather sofa group. "I know who you're lookin' for. I mentioned that on the phone, didn't I?"

"That's right, Mrs. Russo." When the agents had searched Scott Guest's apartment it had been deserted, but his car was still outside.

Having found no clear leads in his home, they had canvassed the area to no avail, but made sure to drop a calling card through the mail slot if no one was home, just to cover all their bases. Mrs. Russo had called later, when they had taken a break for lunch.

"You see, he parks his car underneath my kitchen window nearly every night. That's how I know it's him. Makes an awful racket when he pulls in at night, always disturbing my shows. Would you gentlemen like any refreshments? I pride myself on being a good hostess. My mother always said you should always be ready to serve a three course meal at short notice." She stopped in her tracks and looked back at the agents. "Have you had lunch? I could make you some."

"Oh no, really that's quite alright, Mrs. Russo. We have eaten and we don't want to impose. If you'd just answer a few questions, we'll be on our way," O'Neill said.

"Oh, it's no bother at all. Just tea and cake then?"

O'Neill smiled and accepted her hospitality graciously, ignoring Woodroe's look of annoyance. "It will make her feel at ease," he said as she rummaged about in the kitchen.

"Make her talk more freely."

"Don't think that's one of her problems," Woodroe muttered.

Mrs. Russo returned with tea and a cake covered in chocolate frosting. The two agents were left to perch next to one another on the edge of the small two-seater sofa, each holding a porcelain cup bearing the likeness of a chubby child-like angel.

"I am sorry I don't know his name," Mrs. Russo said. "The one you're looking for. I seem to recall that it didn't really suit him. You know, like a plumber named Beauregard."

"It's Scott, Mrs. Russo. Scott Guest," O'Neill explained.

"Scott? No, that isn't the name I was thinking of at all. Well, anyway he has the same car that my husband used to own. The same model I mean. A Crown Victoria. Except he doesn't seem to know much about cars, does he? He should clean his carburetor out, the amount of noise he makes. Sal—that's my late husband. Sal knew how to keep a car in shape. He could work miracles with any kind of mechanism, my Sal. Car engines, air conditioner compressors, plumbing, whatever the problem, Sal could fix it."

"Uh, is there anything else you could tell us about Scott Guest, Mrs. Russo?"

Mrs. Russo went on, oblivious to O'Neill's question. "I could never mistake that car for anything else, you know. The number of times it's interrupted Barney Miller with that awful backfiring, I'm surprised I don't dream about the thing. That's how I knew it was his when I saw it."

"Outside the kitchen?" O'Neill asked.

"No, no." She waved her hand in dismissal. "Out where my sister lives. She's in a home, see. She's only got ten years on me, the old thing, and still she's already given up her independence like that. Won't catch me moving into a home without a fight. They steal your things, you know. I gave her a beautiful porcelain angel last Christmas and now she can't find it anywhere."

"What was that about the car, Mrs. Russo?"

"Oh, I recognised it instantly. As soon as I got off the bus and saw it. Parked near a white house. At first I thought I was seeing things. What would a young punk like that, incapable of keeping his own car in order, be doing at a nice house like that? Then I think that maybe he's one of them gigolos. He has that unkempt bad-boy look that some ladies find appealing, I guess. You know, like James Dean, only not as handsome. Real people never are, you know. As handsome as movie stars I mean, on account of them being real people. Anyway, then I thought maybe he was visiting his mother, though he didn't really seem the family type." She whispered this last while leaning close to O'Neill and patting him on the knee.

"Where was this?" O'Neill cut in as Mrs. Russo sipped her tea.

"Didn't I say? It was right near the bus stop."

"Which bus stop?"

"The one near the nursing home, of course."

"And where is the nursing home?" O'Neill asked patiently.

"On the corner of Havell Street and Narragansett in Ossining. It's not a very good location. She could have done much better. Picked a place with a view. That's all she does, you know, stare out the window. You'd think she'd *want* a better view. That and play canasta."

"But you're certain it was his car?" Woodroe interrupted, eliciting a glare from the old woman, followed by a triumphant smile.

"Yes, I am. It was still there when I came

back from my visit, but while I was waiting for the bus, he comes out of the house with two other men and gets into the car. Some young lady waves them off. So I think to myself that they can't be...for hire. She looked far too nice to have to resort to that kind of thing. Anyway, I mean three of them? What in god's name would you do with three? Anyway, they all get into his poor car and drive off, making that awful racket."

"Did you get a good look at the men who were with him?"

"Not really."

"Would you mind looking through some pictures?" O'Neill asked, gesturing for Woodroe to get out the folder.

II

"That'll be the stop," Woodroe said later as O'Neill turned onto Narragansett. They could see the house Mrs. Russo had been talking about and that the parking spaces in front of it, where the old lady had claimed to have seen Guest's car, were empty.

"Here we are then." O'Neill said. "I'm

getting a certain Desperate Housewives feeling here, know what I mean? You can bet some strange things go on behind closed doors here. No signs of any of the suspects, though."

Woodroe just grunted and parked just past the junction. "We should get Moretto before he skips," he said, repeating his sentiment from earlier. "Old bat sounded pretty confident when she ID'ed his pic."

"We need more than the ID of one old lady to go on. Maybe we can get some corroboration from the neighbours. Mrs. Russo said she saw the car parked around here on several occasions when she was visiting her sister, so if Moretto and this third guy was with him every time, someone else must have noticed them too. Let's check out the house first, though." He removed his seatbelt and opened the passenger door and Woodroe soon followed.

III

"Oh dear!" Sue sat looking at the email that had just appeared in her mailbox despondently.

Scott glanced up from watching over Finley, who was reclining in a motel armchair wearing their experimental visor. "What's up?" he asked.

She carried the laptop over to him and together they watched a video attachment containing footage of two men in serious suits walking up to her front door.

"FBI?" Scott said without hesitation.

Sue nodded. "I think these are the same guys that visited Frank's place when I was there. Looks like they've managed to connect you to me already."

Scott reached out to restart the movie file. "Yeah. They're good. We'll have to get rid of your car as soon as possible." He looked over at Finley who seemed to be relaxed and breathing normally. "You think it's safe to bring him out early?"

Sue gave Finley a wistful look. She had been trying repeatedly to see the things he could see in the green mists, but somehow it was eluding her. She could feel the sense of space alright, and once she thought she saw...something—or someone, she wanted it so much to be someone —moving around in there. Part of her was beginning to fear that this was just one of Finley's notions, that the green mists were just activating his overactive imagination. "I don't think it makes any difference when we bring him out," she said.

Scott powered down the connection to the entanglement and Finley slowly removed the visor, eyes glowing with excitement. "I think they're trying to talk to me!" he exclaimed. "And there's—"

"Those FBI guys have been to Sue's place," Scott interrupted. "We need to change cars and get moving."

Finley sobered up immediately and started to pack up the visor and connecting cables. While Scott went to the bathroom to get his things, Sue watched Finley pack, knowing that they were in a hurry but unable to tear herself away. She wanted to ask him what he had been about to say. What had he seen this time? He had promised to try to figure out if one of the figures was her uncle or not. Surely he would have told her if he had? When Scott came back from the bathroom, she got herself under control and managed to intercept him before he unceremoniously dumped their collected toiletries into a single pile on one of the beds. As she carried her things back to her bed, Finley was zipping up the backpack where they kept the IPAS.

"I'm sorry you didn't get to take your turn. Maybe we could set something up in the car, once we get the new one?"

"Won't that risk damaging the equipment?"

Finley shrugged. "The drives are solid state so the only thing that could be upset by travelling is the entanglement and with that, it doesn't much matter if the machine is on or off, really. It's still at the same risk. I could probably rig something that'd make it just as safe as in the trunk."

She smiled. "Thank you, Finley, but don't you think sitting in the passenger seat wearing a high-tech visor while going down the interstate might be drawing attention to ourselves?"

Finley looked disappointed. "Yeah, you're probably right." He lifted the bags carefully up on the bed. "I could have made it work though." She heard him mumbling to himself.

TWELVE

I

Darius's day was shaping up to be one of the worst ever. He was still reeling from learning of Kim's previous ties to the hackers, and now Igor had called him as he was getting ready to leave for the lab to tell him that Potter had taken ill during the night and been rushed to hospital. Potter's wife Sandra had requested that Darius join her at Johnson Memorial Medical Hospital and he had spent the entire drive there wondering why. The thought occurred that she might be blaming Potter's condition on the lab or his late night sessions with the experimental device and he wasn't sure she would be wrong to do so. He cursed and hit the steering wheel.

He should never have let Potter tinker with that thing.

After making his way up to Potter's room, Darius had found Sandra sitting next to the bed where her husband lay with various sensors trailing from his body. Darius couldn't help but think Potter looked remarkably like he did when using the virtual equipment.

"How is he doing?" Darius asked in a whisper, closing the door behind him. Potter's wife, startled by the sound of his voice, soon relaxed when she recognised him. "Do they know what's wrong yet?" Darius walked to the opposite side of Potter's bed and looked down at him.

"One of the doctors mentioned something about radiation poisoning," she said.

"Radiation? How is that even possible?"

Sandra gave him a sad smile. "It isn't. The other doctor immediately asked me to overlook that comment, saying there were no signs of radioactivity. They just can't tell for certain what caused this." She paused for a moment then looked into his eyes. "I know, Darius. I know what he's been doing at work. He's told me everything about the quantum internet and his own experiments."

"Has he?"

"You don't need to worry, I'm not blaming you for anything," Sandra continued, before once again looking down at her husband. "He was always too eager for sciences' secrets. You couldn't have stopped him from using the interface even if you'd tried."

She indicated that Darius should sit down and they both drew up their chairs close to the bed. "If my husband has one quality beyond any other, I'd have to say it's his loyalty. He made it perfectly clear that it was his own idea. That no one forced him to do anything." She held Potter's hand in her own, squeezing it. "Anyway, he had been feeling strange for a few days. He said it was just because he was tired, but I could tell it had him worried. He was still awake when we rushed him here. He made me promise to tell you everything."

"Everything about what?" Darius asked.

"'Everything is not as it seems,' he said. Apparently, there are things going on inside your quantum internet." Sandra looked a little uncomfortable. She dropped her eyes from Darius and gazed at her husband before she continued. "There are people inside it."

II

Darius left the hospital much later, after having talked to the doctors. He was staggered by Potter's condition and what he had asked Sandra to tell him. It wasn't hard to understand why Potter had been reluctant to keep notes on his computer after the hack, but he couldn't figure out why he would have kept things secret from all of them. With the loyalty of one of his own employees in question, however, Darius admitted he himself wasn't sure how much of what Sandra had told him he should reveal to the others.

Arriving at the lab, he called the team together and attempted to describe the nature of Potter's condition.

"It seems his hippocampus is enlarged. That's the suspected reason behind his blackout, anyway. Until they've had a chance to go over the results of some secondary scans, none of the doctors seemed willing to speculate any further."

"Well, I think we all know what's caused it, whatever it is," Ray declared. "Has he discussed his virtual work with Sandra? Is she aware of what he's been doing these past few weeks?"

Darius gave a sharp nod. "He's told her everything."

"And she doesn't feel inclined to bring the matter to the doctors' attention? Won't they need to know?"

"Potter asked her not to," Darius replied. "Sandra understands the significance of what he's been doing. And as she said to me, nobody knows for sure what's wrong with him so there's no way to tell if it has anything to do with his research."

"Don't you think the doctors need to make that decision for themselves. They'll need the facts, though? What if they administer the wrong treatment?" Ray persisted.

"And what do you suggest we tell them?" Tony asked. "It isn't like we understand any of this ourselves."

"Sandra's probably right, Ray," Kim agreed. "Or rather Potter is, I guess. None of us know for certain that his experiments are responsible for what's happening to him."

"How about this? Let's just give the doctors some basic information about the experiments he was conducting. Nothing too specific, and nothing about the quantum internet that would violate our NDA with Bionamic," Darius added.

"We need someone to prepare a short summary of Potter's work that we can present to the hospital."

Kim's hand shot up. "I'm not doing anything at the moment."

Darius hesitated, not sure how much responsibility he should place in her, but not wanting her to suspect that he knew about her connection to the hackers. In the end though, the visor and the resonance feedback were Bionamic's secrets and he was getting less and less interested in protecting those. "Okay. Get Dave to help explain what exactly Potter has been up to."

Dave had been sitting in morose silence while the others talked, and started when he was mentioned by name. He agreed with a nod, but said nothing. Darius guessed he was feeling guilty for encouraging Potter to set up the experiments in the first place. *It will do him good to help out,* "the rest of you, just hang tight in the meantime. Igor, I need to speak to you about something else."

Igor joined Darius in his office a few moments later, looking almost as troubled as Darius felt. "What are we going to do?"

Darius logged into his computer and after a

second or two, classical music filled the room.

"Turn away from the windows when you speak," he said, eyes intent on the screen.

Igor's eyes widened. "Am I missing something here?"

Darius directed Igor's attention to the street outside with a discreet nod towards the window. "We have company."

He moved rapidly across the room and looked down at the street between the blinds. "Who—?"

"Woodroe's techies, I suspect. The van, the white Dodge."

"Are you sure?" He turned back towards Darius. "You think they are— That they're listening in right now?"

"Doubtful. Probably not."

Igor silently stared at the tall van parked on the other side of the street for several seconds and described the vehicle as unspectacular. "So what do we do?" he asked, heading back across to Darius' desk.

"About Potter or Kim?"

"About Potter. Do you think he'll be okay?"

"I'm not sure what to think anymore. Sandra seems to think he'll make a full recovery, but I can't help believe that's just wishful thinking on her part. The doctors asked if his duties at Sytek included any work with radioactive materials! Radiation poisoning. People don't easily recover from that."

Igor gaped in dismay. "What exactly are they suggesting we're doing over here. Radioactivity, really!"

Darius shook his head. "Relax. They're doing more tests. That's not the opinion of the senior staff, or frankly our main problem. Potter's been holding out on us about his experiments."

"Is this what you wanted to talk about? Is it something you can't share with the others?"

Darius shrugged and looked helpless. "Potter obviously feels as though it is, possibly with this security leak in mind. I just don't know."

"I met her last year. I've met Sandra twice now and on both occasions she struck me as being highly intelligent."

"Add to that extremely understanding," Darius continued. "The other reason he might not have wanted to say anything is because he thinks we'll all accuse him of going crazy. He's been seeing figures in the feedback. He thinks they're trying to tell him something but he can't make out what they're saying or for that matter what they look like."

Igor eyed him sceptically. "They didn't give you any strange pills over at the hospital this morning, did they?"

"I wish. Maybe then I'd be able to relax. And before you ask, Sandra didn't appear crazy in any way. I don't know if Potter imagined it, but he's certainly convinced her that they are real and she doesn't strike me as the type who's easily taken in."

"So who else knows?"

"Well, obviously those two, can you imagine their dinner chat, us, and probably a handful at Bionamic, if their research ever went as far as ours."

"Ah, back to the infamous Professor Young," Igor theorised. "Do you think Potter managed to turn up any information on that?"

"For all we know, Professor Young could have put some of it in his notes somewhere. If Potter thought this was something Bionamic was keeping from us, then perhaps that would be another explanation as to why he could only discuss it with his nearest and dearest. I wonder how Max is going to respond, or if we should even tell him. If he's aware, then trying to exonerate himself from involvement with the hack is one thing, withholding information that could be vital to the safety and wellbeing of my employees is quite another matter."

"Have you considered that maybe hiding all this from the 'boys outside' isn't the right thing to do?" Igor replied, glancing across at the window. "I'm not sure we're equipped to handle any of this, really."

Darius shrugged again. "And what could the FBI do about the situation?"

Igor sighed. "I just wish that someone would force Max Kohler to tell it straight for once."

Darius gave him a wistful smile. "You and me both."

III

After their previous day's success, Woodroe and O'Neill were still on something of a roll. Sue Young's Lincoln had been found in the short-term parking lot in Waterbury, Connecticut's small airport. They headed there immediately from Ossining and were met at the airport by a local deputy.

"Here we go," Deputy Craig said pointing to the black Lincoln Navigator. O'Neill studied it with interest and the deputy went on. "You really lucked out on this one. If he'd parked in the long-term lot, we probably would never have noticed it at all."

O'Neill could understand how it might have seemed like a good place to dump an unwanted vehicle. Hiding in plain sight among a bunch of other empty cars.

When they reached the Lincoln, O'Neill compared the license plate to the information he had gotten from the DMV about Sue Young's car. He nodded to Woodroe. "This is the one. Check if they left a door unlocked on the other side?"

They tested all the door handles, but everything seemed to be locked down tight. Woodroe looked in through the back window and then stepped back and shrugged. "Cleaned out, anyway," he said.

"You're right," O'Neill agreed after checking through the side windows. "We'll call in a tow and have this transported over to forensics. If there is anything of value in there they'll let us know." He turned to the deputy. "Did anyone notice the car being parked?"

"I don't rightly know. Most of our people are overseeing the damn city parade so I'm afraid I'm it for personnel assigned to this. It's the same every year, ties everybody up."

"If they suspected we were on to them, they would have wanted to get rid of their old car as soon as possible. Which means they probably found their new ride somewhere relatively close by. Now all we need do, is see if we can find out where from."

"I might have someone who can help you with that," the deputy volunteered.

"Someone" turned out to be the sheriff's personal secretary, who, according to the deputy, had the organisational skills of a queen bee.

O'Neill refrained from pointing out that bees are organised by instinct not skill and just accepted the help. The FBI had access to almost every database that could be helpful of course, but there was no way to be sure that the transaction they were looking for had made its way into the registers yet, if there had been any paperwork at all.

Together they went through all the latest ads for cars in the local newspaper, calling each person and asking if the car had been sold yet, and if so, to whom. O'Neill figured they could rule out any new car lots or auction sales, since the suspects wouldn't want their names known and they had abandoned their car, rather than having traded it in. They concentrated on used and plain vehicles, as these would have the kind of low profile that would appeal to people on the run. They were aware that their efforts were a long shot and that their best hope for success would be when the official records of the DMV had caught up with the sale in the next few days.

As the secretary contacted the surrounding newspapers' classified desks, O'Neill and his partner waded their way through likely online sources. O'Neill suffered a momentary flashback from when he'd been a junior agent and stuck with the research jobs that the senior agents no longer had to do. If Woodroe was having similar memories he didn't say.

When he was about to suggest they break for lunch, he noticed Woodroe had stopped reading and was listening to the secretary's phone conversation. When O'Neill raised an eyebrow, Woodroe lifted a finger to his lips.

"Yes. Thank you for your cooperation, you've been most helpful." She put the phone down and turned to the two agents, flipping back to the previous page of her notebook. "I have a lead for you. The editor of the Hartford

Courant told me about a customer who had sold their car through an ad in the paper. Apparently the police had no real interest in what they had to say though. I just finished talking to the people who placed the ad." She adjusted her reading glasses and looked at her notes. "They sold a Volvo, an S80, to a young couple who insisted on paying in cash. Mrs. Wong told me that they seemed to be in a rush. She also mentioned that the young man had suggested that the car was to be a present for his wife, but in the end it was she who gave them the money."

"I don't suppose they happened to notice what kind of vehicle they arrived in?" O'Neill asked.

"They didn't, but Mr. Wong's brother did. He lives just around the corner and saw the couple step out of a black Lincoln Navigator," she continued. "The Wongs live in Newington. It's about a forty-minute drive from here. I told them to expect you."

Woodroe stood up and jingled his keys.

THIRTEEN

Another car, another town, another hotel room, and for Finley, another opportunity to explore the resonance feedback.

Wow. I don't know if I'll ever get used to this. I'm not sure I want to, he thought, once again finding himself staring around the inner walls of a giant pyramid-shaped room. The place seemed much sharper this time. Finley stood some ten feet away from the nearest wall, its emerald green surface had engaged his eye with a glittering spectacle of tiny sparks. The leaning walls disappeared up over him, presumably coming to an apex at some unseen point far above.

On previous visits, he had noticed several transparent patches appearing on the walls, gradually increasing in size with each subsequent visit, giving glimpses of things beyond the confines of this room. Now the walls resembled green radiant glass. Once his eyes had adjusted to the sudden clarity extending beyond the room, he froze as the true majesty of his surroundings revealed themselves.

Left, right, up, down, more and more pyramid-shaped rooms popped into view all connected in an intricate web of touching surfaces. In every direction the transparency opened up the sort of views more associated with a mountaintop vista. A deep rumbling noise began. A bass note unlike anything he had ever heard. As he turned to take it all in, he came face to face with a man. Not a blurry figure as before, but an actual human shape, standing at an impossible angle on what looked to be the other side of the wall Finley was facing. The rumbling noise had faded and was lingering just at the edge of hearing. He ignored it as he tried to take in the idea of this person defying gravity in this very Escherian way. Between the two of them, glowing with an unwavering tone, the wall blazed with a green lustre, and the man's features, in accordance with the angle at which he stood, remained indistinct.

"Can you hear me?" Finley called out, as he had on previous occasions.

The man stepped back and, lifting his left foot onto the angled surface behind him, which would be his wall and more in line with the angle of Finley's floor, proceeded to support his bodyweight with outstretched hands, now firmly held in place against the wall between them. Readjusting his balance, the stranger once again stood upright, no longer resting his hands against the wall. Defying the logic of any normal world, the man stepped through the wall and onto the floor on which Finley was standing, breaching the glass-like divide as though it didn't exist.

Soap bubbles... Well, soap pyramids. Green, radioactive soap pyramids. That's what the whole thing reminded him of.

"Don't worry," he began, speaking with an irrefutable English accent. "You're in no immediate danger here, not from us."

"You're English!" Finley said.

"That's correct, and you are American?"

"I am," Finley replied, looking at the wall

the other man had just stepped through. "Is ignoring physics a family trait? Or is it a skill you developed on your own?"

"Oh, that. You get used to that, after a while, it's not nearly as daunting as it might seem." He smiled and held up a hand in greeting. "My name is Mathew. My friends call me Matt."

"Finley," Finley said bemused.

"He means that he wishes they did. Mostly we call him Mathew," a voice behind Finley said. He spun around to see an older man standing on the other side of the room. The old man too had spoken with an English accent, but seemed more aloof.

"It's good to finally meet you, Finley," the older man continued. "At long last. We were starting to lose faith." Ambling across the room, the man had a certain presence Finley couldn't quite put his finger on. A sort of tired determination that could easily have been mistaken for surliness. *Now this is a man with a mission.* Finley thought.

"At last?" he replied. "Am I to assume you've been watching me?"

"Along with the others. Of late, we've had a profusion of visitors, isn't that right, Mathew? None of whom, it would seem, have taken the trouble to read any of our supplementary research notes."

"You'll have to forgive Melvin, Finley," Matt said. "We've been here so long, that at times it feels like it has been forever."

"Yes, in fact I'm having difficulty keeping track of the months, and years. Mathew might know, eh, Mathew?" the elder man asked.

He smiled. "It's so easy to lose count. Is there any news from our families?" Finley didn't know what to say and Mathew studied him closer. "How are you connected to the project Finley? Is it still ongoing?"

"I'm not part of any project," Finley said. "But the last I heard, the quantum internet tests were proceeding. There is a slight hold-up at the moment but they should continue—"

"The quantum internet! What about the study of the resonance feedback? Was it completed?" Mathew demanded.

"I don't know. As far as I know, I'm the only one doing these trips. Well, apart from a friend, but she's having some troubles experiencing the full glory of it." He gestured at the room and everything surrounding them.

"You are wrong," the older man said. "And you should tell your friend to stop."

"Why?"

"Walk with me," he said, turning around and walking towards the wall he had entered from. Matt fell into line beside Finley as he followed.

"Are you the only ones here?" Finley asked, trying to distract himself from the fact that it looked like he would soon be expected to walk through a wall.

"There is one more of us. Patrick. Then there is—" He gestured in the direction that they were travelling. "Well, you will see soon enough."

The old man reached the wall and stepped through it, walking up the slope on the other side of the wall as if it was flat ground. Finley hesitated, then stopped before the wall. "Will this Patrick join us?" he asked Mathew.

Mathew smiled and stepped through the wall. "He already has."

Confused by the others' words, Finley followed him, placing one foot through the wall and onto the sloping surface on the other side. To his surprise, and at first assuming it be a reflection, he noticed the outline of another shoe met the surface below. Another man stepping onto the underside of this new floor, matching his feet to the spot, almost knocked Finley off balance. He stepped through the wall, looking down at the new floor where Patrick was mimicking his steps. The man then leant forward, grinning and waving, but Finley instinctively stepped away as Patrick, because this must be him, arched his body forward, reaching his arms through the floor, pulled himself through.

"There is no real direction here, no real solidity either, other than what we imagine," Mathew explained.

Eventually dragging his legs and feet into the room, Patrick stood up, approached Finley with an outstretched arm in order to shake his hand, and smiled. Finley returned the gesture, but as his hand passed straight through that of Patrick's, he speedily withdrew his arm in horror.

"Oh, I'm sorry," Patrick grinned. "I couldn't resist," he added, laughing quite a bit louder than Finley thought warranted by the joke. "Couldn't resist!" he persisted. "Get it?" he asked. Finley could only nod lamely. "So who sent the yank?" Patrick suddenly enquired, all the friendliness in his voice abruptly turning into hostility.

Finley turned to look at Mathew. "Who cracked his egg?" he asked. Patrick emitted a low growl.

"Stop it, the both of you," Melvin said. "Patrick's question is a fair one however. Perhaps you might care to edify us with a more convincing explanation of how you come to be here Finley? And shine some more light on the quantum internet? You don't work for Bionamic, that is clear enough." He resumed his walking and Finley hurried to catch up and walk beside him.

"You're Melvin Young, aren't you?" Finley asked. "Professor Young? The same person who worked at the ECSD?"

"I founded it!" Young proclaimed. "But you are avoiding the question. How did you get access to the resonance feedback?"

"Well..." Finley hesitated.

"I think we've got ourselves a hacker here!" Patrick exclaimed. "That's where this one fits in. Hacker or spy." He added, daring Finley to argue that he wasn't. "Or both," he concluded.

"Only a hacker," Finley said, deciding he had nothing to gain from being duplicitous, even if it was one of his favourite words. Anyway it wasn't as if these people were in any position to tell on him. "We were looking for you in fact, Professor."

"Me?" Professor Young sounded genuinely surprised. "I could understand Bionamic trying to recover my knowledge, but an outsider? Whatever for?"

"Well, I'm just in it for the ride, really. Sue is the motivating force."

"Sue?"

"Yeah, your niece. She never gave up looking for you. She couldn't access the secrets of Bionamic directly so she asked for our help to get access to the quantum connection. That's what your efforts have created. Bionamic are planning a worldwide launch."

Finley thought he could see a proud smile on the features of the old man, alongside the mental bruising encountered in this place, which seemed to have taken its toll on the lot of them. "But how did you find out I was here? I imagine that such information would be tightly guarded by Bionamic."

"We didn't know. We found the information on your prototype interaction device, along with some notes on the resonance feedback, while we were looking for information about you. It was just too tantalising not to poke into.

This place is as pristine as a cave echo! Probably as impossible to understand, I expect. It's just amazing in here."

"Then you don't know anything about the things that led up to it," he concluded. "And nothing about the side effects?"

"What side effects?"

"The ones which incarcerate us within this, amazing, place. This whole project has been most irregular. It all started with an artefact. Our basic information comes from an ancient Burmese artefact, did you know that? An artefact with strangely modern scientific notation carved into it. Bionamic's first foray into quantum entanglement came from this item. Not to use it for anything practical, but to examine the feedback effect that it predicted. Ah, here we are." Professor Young said, coming to a full halt.

Finley looked around and found that they had stopped in a room indistinguishable from the one he had first found himself in except that there was an indistinct human shape floating in the air before them. "Who's he?"

"Another visitor," Young explained. "I take it you don't know him then?" Finley shook his head. "No, well, he showed up some time ago.

A few days of normal time."

"Normal time?"

"I knew he wouldn't know!" Patrick yelled.

"Surely you have noticed that the time you spend interfacing with the resonance seems longer to you than the clock tells you? Time is about six times slower here."

"It is!" Finley replied.

"Six-point-oh-one-five-seven-five," Patrick volunteered, nodding as if the exact decimals were of great cosmic importance.

"When we started to examine the resonance feedback, virtually, we noticed some side-effects. Headaches. Tiredness. Nausea. Seizures. We ran tests to understand what was happening and found that our DNA was being damaged."

"Your DNA? How?"

"We couldn't pin it down. Something about the process caused an adverse reaction within the nucleotide chain, resulting in changes which our bodies had trouble handling. We put a stop to the interfacing experiments, against the wishes of the owner, but it was too late. I soon slipped into a coma and the others, well they tell me that the company decided that it would be safest to induce a coma to stabilize their condition." He gestured to the floating form in front of them. "This is how they appeared to me, before they were fully formed."

"Fully formed? You mean it is being grown?"

"Built. By the subconscious of the person it relates to. This man has been interfacing with the resonance feedback on a regular basis. We think he will gain full control of it in a week or two." As if in response to this, the figure in front of them moved its head as if looking around for something. For a moment Finley believed that it was looking at him directly.

"Can he see us?"

"Probably, in the same way you could see us before you came here today. As indistinct figures."

"You had no idea about any of this, did you, Finley?" Mathew asked. "How ironic," he continued. "We thought you were our rescue team and you turn out to be an outsider with no more idea of how to save us than we have ourselves."

"Maybe, maybe not," Young mused. "Are you in contact with Sue, Finley?" he nodded. "Is she the other figure we've been watching?" he confirmed this with another nod. "Then between you you must make every effort to try and contact somebody on the outside for us."

"Isn't that going to be a little difficult. I mean, if I'm now trapped in here, like you, contacting somebody on the outside will be impossible." Finley responded.

"You're different." Patrick said. "You're much more adaptable in here, far more adaptable than we ever were. Far more than he is." Patrick added staring up at the figure before them.

"It's true, Finley," Young agreed. "The man in front of you has been building his body over several weeks, and he is far from done. You on the other hand built yours in a fraction of that. You walked through a wall within moments of your arrival too. I thought you would. It took us several days to learn that trick. It seems likely that you will be able to terminate your experiment and return."

"Well if you're right, and I can, then I'll help!"

"Melvin's usually right," Mathew said. "Have you experienced any of the side effects?"

"No." He shook his head. "But Sue has. Headaches and nausea."

"Which is why you must tell her to stop," Young insisted.

Finley felt his body shake.

"What's happening?" he asked, looking down at himself in surprise as he rocked back and forth slowly.

Professor Young swore under his breath. "Someone is trying to bring you out of the connection. We might have very little time. Listen carefully. There is a room in here that we cannot enter for some reason. We do not know why, but we think it might contain some clues to solving our problem. Also we have no equipment here, no computers, nothing except our own minds. We need help to figure out what is happening. You must contact Professor Arthur Sabatini. Remember. Arthur Sabatini in Phoenix, Arizona. Talk to him and then return to us and tell us what he says."

The crystal constructions around Finley disappeared abruptly and Sue's worried face appeared in front of him.

"Finley!" she exclaimed. "You really had me worried. You wouldn't respond to any of my questions. I was afraid something had happened to you."

Finley sat up slowly, disoriented by the sudden change in environment. "Something did," he modestly declared.

FOURTEEN

I

Kim was having trouble believing what she had just been told. She had gone out for lunch, making sure to pick a particularly noisy place. She pretended not to notice the man following her—probably wouldn't have noticed him if she hadn't expected him to be there—and sat down to eat. Halfway through her meal she had gone to the bathroom to answer a call from Scott. She had tried to ring his number earlier that morning, to warn him and the others about the dangers of using the prototype interface, but had found that his phone was switched off. When she asked him why, he had seemed rushed, and told her that his return call was thanks to Finley who had felt sure that somebody was trying to contact them. So far the call wasn't going the way she had expected.

"What do you mean you already know?" she asked, trying to keep her voice down. "Potter was taken to the hospital only this morning."

Scott made an apologetic sound on the other end of the line. "Someone is in the hospital?" She could hear the voices of Finley and Sue in the background. "Look it's a bit hard to explain, but it fits with some weird things that Finley told us."

"Weird things?"

"Really weird. Look. Maybe you'd better speak with him directly. Hang on."

I'm in a bathroom stall here, remember. Go ahead, feel free to take all the time you need. She wondered how long it would be before her tail became suspicious.

"Hey, Kim. Who went to the hospital?" Finley sounded concerned.

"A colleague. He's the one who's been experimenting with the prototype device on our end. We don't know for sure that it's related, but I thought it was the kind of news you'd need to hear."

"Do you know if there were any symptoms

before he went into his coma?"

"How do you know he's in a coma?"

"Uh... It fits, that's all. Look it's a bit complicated, but Sue is having trouble with nausea and I—"

"Oh no. Really, that's pretty much what Potter was complaining about. Look, you can't keep playing around with that thing."

There were more muffled voices in the background, and then Scott's voice came back on. "Is Potter really in a coma?"

Someone flushed in the stall next to the one where Kim was sitting and she was beginning to feel very exposed. "Yes."

"And his symptoms were the same as what Sue is experiencing?"

"It sounds as though they are. So—" She could hear Sue's voice protesting in the background.

"Look, Kim. I don't quite understand it, but I think we might be out of our depth here. I'll be back in touch soon."

She stared at the silent phone and sighed. Things were rapidly getting out of hand.

II

Checked into a hotel in Hartford, Woodroe and O'Neill awaited news of the whereabouts of the Volvo they'd now confirmed as having been purchased by Sue Young and Scott Guest. Woodroe sat watching the local news on mute while O'Neill spoke to the men in charge of keeping an eye on Sytek.

"And you're sure he was following her? Do we know who he is yet?"

Woodroe could see a frown forming on his colleague's forehead. It was the kind of frown that usually meant more work for the both of them. Woodroe didn't mind more work, but O'Neill tended to become annoyingly energetic when the odds started stacking up against them. He turned off the television and turned his full attention to his colleague's conversation.

"You need to find out who this guy's working for. Just arrest him for interfering with a federal investigation and put some pressure on him. Then bring in the woman and then get the records for that phone. It's time to stop being coy about this."

"Trouble?" Woodroe asked once O'Neill had put away his phone.

"It would seem that someone has been following Kim Knowles."

Woodroe nodded. "Professional?"

"I don't know. She managed to get in touch with her friends without him being any the wiser by slipping into the ladies room, so that tells you how skilled he is. Still, I don't think he's doing it for fun."

"She called them? That a fact?"

"Tried to, they called her back. Our agent overheard most of it. Phone records should confirm it."

"We going back, then?"

"Unless we get another lead here, we might just have to."

Woodroe could see his partner's jaw clench and knew they wouldn't be giving up on finding the others just yet. He lifted the phone and dialled the number for room service. "Coffee?" he asked.

III

Sue woke up in sheets soaked through with sweat, shuddering from cold. She had spent the previous evening trying not to show the others how much her headaches were affecting her. They had already forbidden her from using the prototype device again and Scott was talking about taking her to a hospital. She had gone to bed early, mostly to allay their fears, but once she had pulled up the covers she was kind of glad she had, as she was starting to feel woozier by the minute. One good night's sleep should have made everything alright again. She didn't dismiss everything Finley had told them, some of it she wanted very much to believe, but she couldn't seriously accept she was in danger of being trapped in the resonance feedback. If she wasn't using the device then how could that possibly happen? No, she had been sure she would be in good health again in the morning. She had to be.

Somehow they'd managed to evade the FBI's net so far, but she had a feeling that it was more due to luck than skill, and she was worried that their luck would run out. There was no way they were going to stay ahead if the boys had to play nursemaid as well as avoid the law. Still she took a hot shower and tried to tell herself that she was feeling better. After she got dressed and joined the others, she fired up the laptop to get an idea of the kind of route they would have to take to get to this professor Finley had been talking about. Sue's fingers trembled as they hovered above the keyboard, and she struggled to get them under control.

"You're in no shape for that kind of travel," Scott's voice told her. She turned and found him looking at the laptop screen over her shoulder.

"I'm alright," she mumbled, trying to give him a smile.

"No you're not," Scott said. "You're pale and you're shaking like a leaf. We need to get you to a hospital."

Turning in her seat, she was about to make a heated argument when everything went black. The next thing she knew she was on the carpeted floor looking up at the concerned faces of her friends. "O-kay then," Sue said as Scott and Finley helped her up into a sitting position, the room spinning around her. "I guess I am going to the hospital after all."

She was carried to the car, which she protested against at first, but when her legs wouldn't bear her weight, she reluctantly accepted. After loading their bags, Scott had them out on the highway in no time. Whenever the car made a turn, she could feel nausea coming on, but she didn't say anything. "When we get there, stay in the car while we go get someone."

She shook her head. "No. You drop me off and continue before anyone asks you any questions." She fumbled with her bags and pulled out the money belt that she had been too clumsy to put on that morning, handing it to Finley in the front seat. "Here, this is the cash we've got left. In case you have to get a new car or something. I'll be okay."

"We're not going to leave you on your own," Scott protested. "Besides if it is experimenting with that prototype that got you this way, Finley might be next. I'd much rather he was checked out."

"And just give up? There's no way the feds won't find us if we all check in to the hospital. Then how are any of us getting in touch with this professor Sabatini?"

"We're being noticed,,, there's somebody," Finley said, before turning to indicate a police cruiser fifty yards or so behind them.

"Just act normally," Sue whispered, as they all focused on the approaching car in silence.

"Please be on your way home for breakfast," Scott muttered as the car passed them.

"He's checking the DMV. Could they have connected us to this car already?" Finley asked, half-murmuring the words to himself.

Sue looked at the police car through the front window. She couldn't make out how many people were in the car, let alone what they were doing.

"What? How can you tell they're checking the DMV?"

"Oh no. The car is flagged. Take a left here before he tries to stop us, left here, Scott," Finley insisted.

"How the hell do you know this?" Scott asked, making the turn even as he protested.

"I don't know. I saw it."

"Saw what?" Scott continued. "How the hell. There's no way—"

"I saw it in my mind, okay? It was a flash. Like watching a picture, on TV. He was looking the car up on the on-board computer. I don't know how to explain it but I know it was real. It felt real, like I'd just seen it through a window!"

Sue turned to look out the back of the car, seeing the cruiser entering the street in the far distance. "Finley's right. He's coming alright, He's turned the car around," she said. "How do we get out of this one?"

Finley seemed to be holding his breath, then he said, "We don't. Turn the next corner and I'll get out once we're out of sight."

"You'll do what?" Scott exclaimed. "We're not dumping you—"

"Look," Finley interrupted. "You need to get Sue to the hospital and someone has to go talk to this professor. You know it has to be me because I'm the only one who can reliably bring the information back to Professor Young. So I get out and I make my own way down to Phoenix."

"I don't—" Scott started. This time Sue was the one interrupting.

"Do it, Scott. He's right. It has to be him. If the feds manage to get hold of all of us before we talk to the professor..." she paused. "There's some weird stuff going on, but if there's a chance my uncle is trapped in there and Finley is the only one who can help him escape, I'll do anything to make that happen."

"You've been outvoted, Scott," Finley said. "Now find somewhere out of sight to drop me before he catches up and pulls us over."

IV

"We've got two more," O'Neill said as he put away his phone and resumed control of the car. "The woman, Sue Young apparently got sick. We get the lucky break for once."

"Sick?" Woodroe asked. "Sick how?"

"I don't know. Scott Guest is in custody so maybe he'll tell us. There's another policeman watching the woman over at the hospital."

"What about the other guy?"

O'Neill shook his head. "No sign of him. I'm sure his friends can tell us though."

"Well, that's good."

"Yeah. One thing that does bother me, though. Apparently a very inquisitive man came by the hospital. Tried to talk his way past the guard on the woman's door. Asked a lot of questions at reception. This external interest in the people we are investigating is vexing to me."

Woodroe shrugged. "He comes back, we nab him."

FIFTEEN

I

Climbing into their car outside the hospital, Woodroe and O'Neill watched as Scott Guest was put into the police cruiser behind them. They hadn't been able to take both suspects because of the woman's condition, but a police guard had been left behind and she would be airlifted back to Washington once the doctors decided it was safe.

"Not much of a talker, is he?" Woodroe mused as he pulled out into traffic.

"Very uncommunicative person," O'Neill agreed moodily. "I'm wondering if we should have pushed him harder."

Woodroe shook his head. "Na, take too long.

His friend'll be long gone."

"Yeah, you're probably right. The trooper said that he knew he'd lost one of them, between seeing them and following their car up here, but like he said, what was he supposed to do. The last man must have jumped out with the narrowest of margins at some point."

"With enough time to grab their electronics," Woodroe added. "Now I wonder why he'd do something like that?"

"Maybe there's evidence on their computers they don't want us to have," O'Neill guessed. "Or, maybe, he isn't done using them."

"Perhaps. Not sure he'll get the opportunity now to do that," Woodroe mumbled. "Being on the run all alone."

II

"Ticket please," the collector demanded. Finley took his gaze off the overhead compartment where the laptop and the IPAS were stored and started fumbling through his pockets for his ticket. He found it in his inside jacket pocket, where he had found it the last dozen or so times he looked.

He looked up and down the train car nervously. He had been half-expecting black-suited agents to show up at any moment. The fact that they had not appeared did very little to settle his nerves. Surely they must have been watching the train stations? The ticket collector, however, was not accompanied by any sinister agents of government.

Finley held out his ticket. The collector smiled and looked at it.

"Headed to Phoenix, eh," he said.

"Yeah. Going down to see my brother," Finley improvised.

"Nice weather down there. Dry." The man's voice broke on the last word and he cleared his throat and handed the ticket back. "Sorry. I'm just recovering from a bad cold. Hope you have a good time with your brother."

Finley nodded and put away his ticket. He closed his eyes and rubbed his temples. He was on edge, the ticket collector was on edge, the whole world seemed on edge. If he wasn't going to be arrested he might as well try to get some sleep. He settled back in his seat and tried to relax.

He had almost succeeded in lulling himself to sleep when he suddenly felt lightheaded. He leaned forward, putting his head between his legs to fight the nausea he was sure would come. Sue had been first, he realised. He would be next. But instead of the expected upheaval, Finley suddenly saw an image of the ticket collector speaking into his radio somewhere else on the train. The scene changed to men in black battle gear running up a set of stairs and onto a rooftop where a helicopter was waiting.

The images disappeared, leaving Finley staring down at the train floor. It felt like the visions he had seen in the car, only stronger, more insistent. There were sounds—indistinct and muffled—but still sounds, and smells.

They'll be waiting at the station, he thought. *They'll get there ahead of me and they'll be waiting at the next station. I need to get off this train.*

Finley stood up abruptly, almost hitting his head on his own bags. An old lady in the seat in front of him gave him a look then returned to her romance novel. *Normal. Act normal.* Smiling at a businessman in the seat across the aisle he wiped his hands on his shirt, grabbed the bag with the IPAS and the laptop and headed towards the dining car.

* * *

"News?" Woodroe asked O'Neill just off the phone, frowning.

"Our final suspect's on a train heading south. We'll have police search it at the next stop."

"Good." Woodroe looked over at his partner who looked anything but happy. "Not good?" he ventured.

"I'm not sure. Apparently someone had already been asking around at the station, claiming to be with the agency."

Woodroe looked at the police car behind them in the rear-view mirror. "Turn back?"

O'Neill shook his head. "No. The police are taking every precaution. If anyone else tries to grab him, they'll take them in as well."

"You sure?"

"Yeah. We have to focus on the suspects we have. These new guys are obviously amateurs. If any of the official teams had been in on this, we'd know." O'Neill drummed his fingers impatiently on his leg. "We don't have time to mess with them."

Woodroe shrugged.

* * *

The dining car was curiously empty for a long trip like this one, though Finley imagined that the quality of the food might have something to do with it. A glass of watery beer and a limp BLT stared back at him from the table as he tried to think of what to do next. It was obvious he needed to somehow slip away before the next station, but jumping off a train at full speed would be suicide and pulling the emergency stop would attract a lot of attention he couldn't afford.

He shut his eyes as a sudden pressure in his head heralded what he thought would be another headache. Instead there was the train. As if he were high up and far away from it. There was a brief but overwhelming sense of vertigo before he realised he was not flying. He could still feel the bite of sandwich in his mouth, the bench he was sitting on against his thighs. Yet his vision was somewhere far above and behind his body, watching the tiny train far below. The tiny train and a small black spot somewhere behind it.

The world sped past in the blink of a second and suddenly he was much closer, looking down at a black helicopter as it raced to catch up with the train. Inside the helicopter there were men. Men looking for him. He didn't know how he knew, but he knew it was the truth.

He snapped his eyes open, and moved to stand, accidentally knocking over his not-quite-empty beer glass, tripping on his bag and banging his knee against the table at the same time. Ignoring the pain, Finley shuffled out from his seat, giving the young cashier an apologetic grin.

"I'm really sorry," he said. "Do you mind cleaning that up for me? I have to go."

He turned, grabbed his bag off the floor, and walked back through the connecting doors to the next train-car, ducking out of sight as soon as the doors closed behind him.

To his right, through the window of the outer door, the one not leading to a safe train car, the landscape was flashing by at enormous speed. It seemed impossible that he would be able to get off at this speed and survive, but his whole situation seemed impossible. He was on a train being chased by a helicopter. He couldn't think of any reason for this that didn't involve action that belonged in a movie rather than real life. And if there was movie-grade madness going on, well then perhaps jumping off a moving train was the lesser of two crazies. He reached out and opened the train-car door. The clunking sounds of the train on the tracks became louder and were joined by the sound of the wind rushing past outside. *Although, if you think about it, the train is moving through the wind. Or even more accurately both the wind and the train are moving past each other. Or—*

Finley cut the thought off and leaned his head out to look ahead in the direction the train was moving. They were coming up on a wooded area, trees and undergrowth whooshing towards him at however many miles an hour the train might be moving.

Well, that's convenient. Soft undergrowth to land in, if I'm lucky. Or a tree trunk to hit my head on if I'm not.

He climbed down the steps, on the irrational idea that perhaps it would hurt less if he were closer to the ground. He looked back into the safety of the moving train and then down onto the ground speeding past. He shrugged the bag off his shoulder and let it swing back and forth, feeling its weight before letting go. He had time to see the bag disappear among the trees before it was out of sight. There was no way to tell if it had survived or not.

He closed his eyes. He regretted having let go of the bag now. He hadn't really decided that he would jump until he threw the bag; he could still have backed out at any moment. Now he couldn't.

Aw, hell! he thought and let go of the train.

He hit the embankment rolling, the world a kaleidoscope of forest colours, then he stopped abruptly as something stood in his way. The wind was knocked out of him and the pain made him black out for a few seconds, but unless the helicopter had circled around, it had only been the briefest moment because he could still see the chopper in the sky, following the train.

He ignored the pain and rolled into the shelter of the trees and bushes. As soon as the helicopter had passed overhead Finley gritted his teeth, got up on his hands and knees and crawled further into the undergrowth.

SIXTEEN

I

"What is this about?" Kim asked, eyeing the two FBI agents across the table from her. "Darius, what's going on?"

"Mr. Daucourt is present only as an observer, Ms. Knowles. This conversation will chiefly be between you, me and Mr. Woodroe here," O'Neill, the shorter of the two agents, told her.

"Mostly him, though," Woodroe said.

O'Neill gave his colleague a quick look before returning his gaze to Kim. "We have Scott Guest in our custody, ma'am. He was captured along with Susan Young."

Kim felt the muscles at the corner of her eye

twitch and her mouth go dry. She had not heard anything from Sue or the others for more than 24 hours and had been afraid that something had gone wrong.

"Before you deny your connection to these people, I want to inform you that because of your ties to Scott Guest and the evidence we have so far collected against him and his associates, I have managed to obtain a court order for your cell phone and any personal electronic devices, including any laptops or other computers. In fact, I believe we could collect your microwave if we were so inclined."

O'Neill then placed a familiar-looking smartphone on the desk between them. "This is Susan Young's telephone. You're no doubt aware that it's rigged up to send untraceable messages to an anonymous receiving email address. Now, do you suppose if I send a message from this," he pointed at the phone, "and that message winds up on one of your devices, that I could convince a judge of your involvement in all of this?"

Kim just stared down at the table, imagining that her face was going pale and that her ears were burning red. She took a breath and looked up. "I'm sorry, Darius. We were never after

Sytek. We only wanted to expose Bionamic."

"And did you?" Darius asked.

"Yes." She sat up straighter in her seat. "Yes, we did. Sue's uncle is in a coma in one of their facilities and they're trying to cover it up. Now they're tricking your people into doing their research for them and Potter slips into a coma as well. I told you Bionamic was bad news, Darius. They'll do anything to get what they want. You have to see that."

II

Darius watched the back of Kim's head as she exited the office they had used for an interrogation room, wondering why the agents had asked that he remain behind.

"Do you believe her?" O'Neill asked him once they were alone.

Darius found himself nodding slowly. "Yes. I know I shouldn't but I do. I mean... It's all a lot to take in, but the weirder bits I've already heard from Dave and Potter. And the rest, well... I do believe she never meant to hurt Sytek. There is no evidence that any sensitive information was removed from our offices. The only thing stolen was a cluster of entanglements, and since the other half of that system is across the ocean it was clearly not an attack on *this* establishment."

"And Bionamic kidnapping people and covering up information? Using your staff as guinea pigs?"

Darius shook his head in bewilderment. "I don't know. I wouldn't have thought that was the kind of thing *anyone* would actually do, but I've never encountered anyone like Max before. If there really is a connection between Potter's status and his experiments, and Max knew about the dangers before sending us the information and that experimental device, well then I think he might be capable of just about anything." He looked O'Neill in the eyes. "Is she right?"

O'Neill straightened his tie. "We try to draw our conclusions from the facts at hand Mr. Daucourt. At the current moment, there isn't anything conclusive to say whether Ms. Knowles is correct. There are, however, a number of circumstantial factors and incidents that seem to indicate that Bionamic is not dealing with us in complete faith and trust. In fact, we have reason to believe they have solicited the aid of an outside private agency to compete with our attempts to bring in the stolen items and information."

Darius shifted his gaze to Woodroe. "Is she right?" he asked again, more insistently this time.

Woodroe shrugged. "Probably," he said.

"That's why we wanted to talk to you. We'd like you to help us find out." O'Neill continued. "We imagine he might be a bit more forthcoming with you."

III

Finley threw the screwdriver down on the bed with a sigh and leaned back in the motel room's only chair. There was no way he was going to be able to fix the dented IPAS, and even if he could, he was pretty sure the entanglement was no longer being contained within. No entanglement, no resonance. No resonance, no way to get back to Professor Young and the others.

He thought about taking another shower. He couldn't really get much cleaner, but the memory of how the hot water had soothed his aching body was calling to him. Jumping off a moving train had not been the most health-conscious choice he had made this decade and almost every part of his body protested despite the non-prescription painkillers he was going through like candy.

At least he was reasonably sure that nothing important was broken. He was not leaking blood from anywhere and he could move all of his limbs in a reasonable manner. When he had first gotten up and started to look for the bag with the laptop and the IPAS, he had been certain he was going to discover that he was bleeding internally at any moment, or that his legs would give out, a broken bone poking out through the skin like some demented junior surgeon's idea of a jack-in-the-box.

The trek through the woods once he had found the bag had been equally painful, the visions of immediate disaster having been replaced by a certainty that he would collapse before he reached civilisation. He had climbed over fallen trees, overgrown ruts and slid down muddy inclines. When he finally stumbled out of the woods, he'd found himself at the outskirts of some small town or other.

The cashier at the first drugstore he spotted

kept staring at him as if she was afraid he was going to pull out a gun and rob her, but she sold him a large quantity of medication nonetheless. A careless driver at a gas station had left his keys in the ignition, furnishing Finley with a brand new black Chrysler sedan. It was temporary of course, since he knew it would be reported stolen as soon as he sped out of the gas station, but it allowed him to cover a reasonable distance from the train tracks before anyone started looking.

He had left the Chrysler outside a truck stop café, where he had a greasy meal and hitched a ride with a trucker. He would have walked a couple of miles first, if he could have, to throw off pursuers, but during his short rest all the aches and hurts he had been ignoring had come back with a vengeance to let him know just how much of an idiot he had been to jump off the train in the first place. He had settled for slipping the truck driver a couple of Franklins to forget she had seen him and she kindly dropped him at a motel in the next town down the highway. It wasn't exactly professional spy tactics, but it was the best he could think of on short notice.

This had all led him to spending three hours on a motel chair trying to make sense of the innards of a machine he didn't understand. It was time to admit that the patient was beyond his help. If it was possible to fix it, perhaps Professor Sabatini would be able to help. If not...well, he'd cross that bridge when he came to it.

The next step was to get a new car. Well, actually the next step was to get about two days of sleep, but right after that, a new car.

* * *

There were dreams. They were filled with green haze and strange shadowy figures. Atop a pedestal rested a wooden box covered in modern symbols. As Finley ran his hands over them, they sent a glow up along his fingers, into his body, and disappeared from the wood. The figures all around him gathered closer and nodded at him, then one of them leaned in and whispered in his ear. He smiled. It was all going to be okay. Somehow, it would all work out.

Later, when he woke up, he lay there a moment, wishing he could remember what the figure had told him.

SEVENTEEN

I

"I'm not happy, Darius. Not happy at all," Max said. "This business is throwing off our time-table completely. Your feds are proving to be less than useful as well."

"You mean the ones you called in? The ones who have managed to identify and capture three of the people involved in the hack so far?" Darius replied. He didn't trust Max enough to include Kim in the count. If the other man was playing his own game, Darius didn't want to show any more of his cards than he had to. Also he still had trouble thinking of Kim as one of the bad guys.

Max scoffed. "Maybe. But have they recovered our property? Have they discovered what they know, or who they are working for? I couldn't care less about the people. Sure, I'll be happy to see them rot away in prison, but first and foremost we have to protect the project and the company. These federal agents, they have their priorities all wrong. Luckily it's not just up to them anymore."

"What do you mean?"

"I mean there are other people. People that work for money, not for the American government. People whose priorities I can set. We'll soon have all this straightened out, don't you worry."

Darius was taken aback by the straight admission. The arrogance of the man infuriating him. It was as if Max thought himself invulnerable on the other side of the ocean, immune to any fall-out from his choices.

"You hired a private firm? Damn it, Max, they've been following my people. Did you authorise that?"

"Oh, don't be naïve, Darius. You think your people are above suspicion? I authorised them to do whatever is necessary to locate our property and find out what information has been compromised. My priorities are with the company, Darius. Where are yours?"

"Which company would that be?" Darius asked. "Sytek or Bionamic?"

"If we go, you go, Darius. You must see this. We're in it together. What's good for Bionamic is good for Sytek."

"Really?" Darius asked. "You are seriously asking me to believe that you wouldn't drop Sytek like a hot potato if it meant you could distance yourself from a potential scandal."

"Scandal?" Max asked, squinting at Darius through the screen as though he were sat a few feet away. "What scandal would that be? Who have you been talking to?"

Darius shrugged. "Nothing specific, I only meant—"

"Don't jerk me around, Darius. If you know anything you're not telling me you'd better become very forthcoming very shortly or we *are* going to find ourselves on different sides of the fence. And believe me, you don't want to be on that side of the fence right now."

"Hey. Don't you threaten me," Darius growled. "You're the one who's been holding out, not telling me about this...whatever your private company is called. Don't you dare point the finger at me."

Max scowled from his end of the call and for a moment Darius thought he was going to hang up, then the face split in a wide politician's like grin. "You have a backbone. I like that. Tell you what: I'll send over the reports from the security firm I hired. Then if there is anything you haven't told me I'll be expecting to hear from you. Don't cross me on this, Darius. There's such a thing as being too cocky."

The screen turned dark. Darius ejected the memory stick on which he had recorded the conversation and tapped it thoughtfully against the desk.

II

"What are you doing at the window again?" Sarah Fenwick called out from the back office. "Leave the guests alone!"

Fred Fenwick ignored his wife and continued to peer out through the blinds overlooking the motel parking lot. The door behind him opened and he could feel her presence over his shoulder.

"Are you still trying to spy on that guy in

room five?" she asked. "One of these days, Frederick Fenwick, you are going to creep out the last of your potential guests and that day I'm taking the money and moving to the Bahamas."

"I'm just protecting our investment here," Fred grumbled. "Violent fella, I'd bet. Looked like he'd been in a fight. And did you see the way he was hugging himself? Withdrawal symptoms, I tell you. Do you know what our rooms would look like if we let in every crackhead and speed freak in the area? They'd be trashed. Furniture torn to pieces. Wall-to-wall vomit. Is that the kind of future you want for our establishment?"

"What do you think we are? The Hilton? We can't afford to turn away people during off-season. Anyway, he seemed like a perfectly nice young man when I spoke to him."

Fred scoffed. His wife was wonderful in several ways—at any rate she was adequate where it counted—but she was entirely too trusting. If he had been at the reception desk when that punk came in, he would have sent him packing.

He turned away from the window and tapped his finger at the line in the register where their guest had signed in. He couldn't quite make out what it said. The writing was thin and spidery, making the first name look like Eelux. Just the kind of writing someone would use to cover up who they were.

"What did he say his name was?" he asked.

"Leiter, Felix Leiter," his wife answered. Fred frowned. He had expected some obviously fake name, like John Smith.

"And you checked that his ID matched the name, did you?"

"There was no call for that. He paid in cash."

Fred settled into a satisfied smile. "Cash? And you didn't smell him out as a weirdo? No one but criminals carry around cash these days."

"You do," his wife protested.

"Well, I wouldn't have to if the damn banks could be trusted, would I?" He turned back to the window and peered out at the door to number five. The door opened and the guest inside shuffled out. He looked just as shifty as he had when he checked in the night before. His clothes were crumpled and he was blinking as if he was unused to the light of day. "Anyway," Fred continued. "I'm an upstanding citizen, not a junkie criminal. I should probably tell Lloyd about this one."

"I thought the sheriff told you not to call him anymore."

"Unless it was important, Sarah," he said as he reached for the phone. "He said not to call unless I though it was important."

III

Finley saw the blinds of the motel reception move as he exited his room. He didn't know what he had done to make the proprietor suspicious but it didn't really matter, the damage was done and he could only hope that he would be away from there before the man decided to act on whatever bug had crawled up his exhaust pipe.

When he left the motel, he didn't have a specific plan. Stealing a vehicle would draw too much attention and buying one would leave a paper trail, but his steps led him towards the outskirts of town. He walked along the streets scanning the houses he passed, pleasantly surprised to find that his muscles were starting to hurt less as they limbered up, but worried they would punish him for it later.

As house after house passed him by without presenting him with the opportunity he was looking for, he began to lose focus, just walking without really looking where he was going. After a while, his legs started to protest and he looked around for somewhere to rest. A nearby house had marked the corner of their property with a large white stone and he limped over to it and sat down.

I wish I had brought something to drink. I didn't expect for this to turn into a survival trek.

He leaned back and rested his elbows on the stone, turning his face to the sun.

Weather's nice though.

He opened his eyes and looked up and down the street. It was strangely quiet, the only people along the street being himself and a middle-aged man sitting in a lawn chair two houses down reading a book. The man looked up from his book and nodded at Finley who waved at him.

Finley got up and started to walk over towards the man. There was an old truck on the driveway and a town car in the open garage. There was a dented bucket and a rolled up hose by the truck, the bucket containing a few sponges and some cleaning agents. The man in the lawn chair took a sip of beer, putting down the bottle next to the chair and turning the page of the book.

As Finley came closer, the man folded his book up and put it on the grass next to his beer.

"Nice day, isn't it?" Finley said, hoping his appearance didn't immediately paint him as suspect in the other's mind.

"Sure is," the man agreed.

"Washing your truck?" Finley continued.

The man stared at him from below the brow of his cap. "If I could wash the truck while sitting over here, it would have been done already," he dryly noted.

"Not your favourite job, then?" Finley asked. The man didn't reply, looking like he was waiting for the conversation to be over so he could go back to his book. "You wouldn't have to wash it if you sold it," Finley ventured.

The man raised an eyebrow. "You in the market?"

"Maybe. What's it worth? Twenty-five hundred?"

The man rose from his seat and walked over to the truck, stroking the side of it. "I've had it quite a while now. It's always treated me well.

It's worth at least three, maybe four. Not that I'm thinking of selling."

"What if I offered you ten?" Finley said.

"Ten? Would that be ten thousand dollars?" The man squinted at him. "I'm fond of this truck, but even I would never give ten for it. Why would you?"

"Normally, I wouldn't, but I—" Finley looked at the other man, trying to gauge him, measure him with his eyes. "Look, I'll tell it to you straight. There are people looking for me and I need to get somewhere before they find me. I'd like to buy your truck for a price that will make you agree with me that no paperwork is needed, with enough left over to make you keep the deal to yourself."

The man removed his cap and scratched the back of his neck, looking Finley over from top to bottom. "Who are you running from?"

Finley looked at his shoes. "I'm not a bad man. I'm not a murderer or kidnapper. I don't run drugs or weapons."

"That's not what I asked."

"The FBI," Finley admitted. Somehow it felt good to have said it so openly.

The man smiled. "Then why even bother running? If the feds are after you, surely they're gonna get you in the end?"

"Maybe." Finley didn't want to dispute that point. "Alright, probably." He relented under the man's prying gaze. "I don't intend to keep running forever. I just need to talk to someone before I'm brought in."

"They do give you a phone call you know, when they arrest you."

"I'll give you fifteen," Finley said.

"This would be in the form of a check, I expect?" the man asked. "How can I trust that you're good for it? How can you trust me not to turn around and report the truck stolen as soon as you drive off?"

"I don't think you'd do that. I'm usually a pretty good judge of character. As for you trusting me, I'd be paying you in cash."

"Is that right? Unfortunately I'm not as good a judge of character. I mean, I want to believe you, but usually when I give someone the benefit of the doubt I end up regretting it. Your story is a bit hard to swallow to start with and now you're telling me that you wander around with fifteen thousand dollars' worth of cash on you?"

"Yeah, I know. But it's true." Finley pulled up his shirt, opening up his money belt to show the green inside. The other man stroked his lower lip thoughtfully. Finley counted the money out and held it in his hand. "Fifteen thousand dollars. Clean, honest money, I swear."

"Ah, what the hell. I really didn't want to wash the damn thing anyway."

Finley smiled. When he handed the money over to the man he was surprised that the transaction hadn't left him feeling more unsatisfied.

EIGHTEEN

I

Pulling the cap that the man had thrown in with the truck since "no Chevy driver should be without one" down low, Finley drove at a crawl past the motel making sure it was safe to return. The Jeep Cherokee in the parking lot sporting a sheriff's star on the side told him it wasn't.

He dug into the leg-pocket on his pants as he sped up again and brought out the hard drive he had removed from the laptop and the roadmap he had bought at a gas station. He put the laptop-drive in the glove compartment and tried to unfold the map on the passenger seat while driving. He soon gave up and pulled into a parking space outside a convenience store to be able to figure out exactly where he was and how to get to the highway without crashing into anything.

According to the girl on the telephone directory assistance, which Finley had dialled from a payphone—a bizarre experience in itself in this electronic age, but one necessitated due to the loss of the laptop and in deference to the FBI's ability to trace cell-phone activity— Professor Sabatini could be reached at the university where he lectured at near Phoenix. Finley plotted two possible routes on the map, a faster one that stuck to the major roads as far as possible and a more circuitous one which would keep him on back roads and out of sight. Either way he would be on the road for several days.

He got out of the truck, locking it carefully as it was the only fifteen-thousand-dollar vehicle in the area, and headed for the store to purchase provisions.

II

"Where the hell are you taking me?" Scott demanded as the FBI agents turned from a main downtown road onto a side street.

"You don't recognise it?" O'Neill asked. "You hacked the place."

"Sytek?" Scott asked, looking out at the buildings they passed.

"If we didn't already have you red-handed, Mr. Guest, that was almost as good as a confession right there."

Scott blustered. "Screw you. Of course I knew the name of the company. You've only been saying it every other question the last few days."

"Yes. But you didn't protest your innocence. People who are genuinely innocent tend to be pretty adamant about it."

"There's a limit to how many times you can say the same thing."

"Not really. 'Less you're dead," Woodroe interjected. "Or mute," he added.

Scott tried to burn a hole in the back of Woodroe's head with his eyes, but was distracted by the strangely small sign telling him that the building they just pulled up next to was the home of Sytek. Somehow he had imagined it would be flashier. The building itself was however oppressively non-descript and he found himself starting to sweat.

"What are we doing here?" Scott asked.

"We're going to have a little round table," O'Neill said. "Your chance to tell your side of the story."

"Here?" Scott asked as Woodroe opened his car door.

"Guess who you are going to tell it to?" O'Neill said with a smile.

The walls felt like they were closer than they had to be as Scott was led through the corridors of the building, and he had to resist the urge to drag his feet. At that moment it wouldn't have surprised him if they had dragged him down into a dank cellar never to be seen again. Once they had passed through another door with the Sytek logo, the atmosphere lightened up, concrete giving way to wood panelling and fluorescent lights giving way to recessed wall lighting.

The feeling of relief only lasted for a short while, until they turned a corner and Scott saw Kim sitting in a glassed-in conference room with a man he hadn't seen before. O'Neill's earlier comment suggested to Scott that the man was probably the CEO of Sytek. Although the man was frowning, Scott found him not to be as foreboding as he was expecting. Kim's presence knotted his stomach, though. He was unable to read her expression, but he could only think of one reason she would be here: she had been found out. The agents led Scott through the door to the conference room table and told him to sit down.

"Welcome, Scott," the unknown man said. "I'm Darius Daucourt. I'm sure our friends from the FBI have introduced themselves. And of course you know Kim."

Kim avoided Scott's eyes.

"I know what you're thinking Scott, but Kim didn't sell you out," O'Neill said from Scott's left where he had taken a seat while Woodroe had parked himself in the chair to the right. "In fact, we wouldn't even have known she was involved had it not been for her association with you. With that in mind, maybe we can dispense with the claims of innocence and instead concentrate on your allegations towards Bionamic."

Scott turned to look at O'Neill, expecting the agent to have a superior smirk on his face, but he seemed to be completely earnest. Scott glanced back at Kim who nodded, meeting his eyes this time.

"They're serious," she said. "I've told them about Professor Young and the resonance feedback."

"And they believed you?" Scott asked.

"And about there being what looks like some sort of computer generated dreamland in the particle entanglement," O'Neill's voice buzzed from his left again, "that you can visit virtually. We don't have the science to answer any of that. It sounds like so much bullshit, if you'll excuse my French. Even if it were true, it's not something we have jurisdiction over.

"The CEO of Bionamic being a ruthless bastard who covers up the fact that some of his scientists are in a coma due to unforeseen side-effects of his own technology? And then that he would entice other innocent people to repeat those experiments without warning them of the dangers? That part we are willing to be persuaded about."

Scott licked his lips. "So if we prove to you that we're not the bad guys here... We can walk?"

Woodroe gave a short laugh that almost

sounded like a cough, but it was O'Neill who answered.

"This is not a movie, Mr. Guest. If you turn out to be right, that doesn't mean you didn't already engage in criminal activity when you hacked Sytek's network. The one crime doesn't erase the other." Scott felt his cheeks heat as the agent spoke. "That said, if you cooperate in bringing a case together against Mr. Kohler that would get the attention of the appropriate agencies, a judge might be convinced to be lenient with your sentence."

"Okay," Scott said finally. "I'll give you what we managed to find out, as long as one thing is understood. Frank Moretto was not involved in the hack; he just put together the boxes, he didn't know what they were going to be used for."

Scott looked from one agent to the other, meeting their stony gaze.

"Doubtful," Woodroe stated.

O'Neill, however, gave a curt nod. "At present we don't have any solid evidence linking him to the actual hack. I can't promise he won't be prosecuted if new evidence suddenly presents itself, but if you play nice here, we won't go looking for it."

"Right," Kim's boss said. "So, with that out of the way. Would one of you fine gentlemen of the FBI please tell us what had prompted this meeting."

"Medical report," Woodroe asserted.

"Pardon?" asked Darius.

"Apart from the fact that our confidence in the sincerity of Max Kohler and Bionamic is currently exhibiting a decidedly waning tendency, we have recently received medical evidence that supports there being a common cause for the problems afflicting Susan Young and your colleague Mr. Potter."

"What kind of evidence?" Darius asked. Scott found himself nodding along. This was about Sue now. This was important.

"We have a report from Doctor Havelyn, a medical expert that the bureau consults with on occasion, comparing the cases of Mr. Guest's friend and your physicist and they are remarkably similar."

"Identical," Woodroe grunted.

O'Neill continued, ignoring his partner's comment, opening a file that he had brought with him and reading out points from it. "They both first experienced symptoms after some exposure to the prototype interface device.

They both have symptoms consistent with exposure to radiation without any traces of radiation. They both remain unconscious but there is no indication as to the cause of their comatose state. Apart from what has already been mentioned, they both seem to be in good physical condition, yet all attempts to rouse them have failed. Also they both show signs of an enlarged hippocampus, with much synaptic activity around this region of the brain, where Havelyn believes quantum like activity has been shown to exist.

"However, the only thing Doctor Havelyn is prepared to say with any certainty is that the two cases appear to be related. Certain enough in fact that he has called in the CDC to oversee the matter in case it turns out that the cause is some sort of infection. He refuses to commit to a conclusive diagnosis." O'Neill closed the file. "Which, if you remove the extraneous circumlocution, means that he doesn't know what the hell we are dealing with here.

"Now, according to Miss Knowles's statement, her understanding was that the last of your group, whom she has refused to give the full name of but who we have identified as "Finley" from messages recovered from the mobile phones we confiscated during the arrest of Mr. Guest and Miss Young, has been using the prototype device more frequently than Miss Young without being visibly affected."

"What of it?" Scott asked. He was beginning to suspect he knew where this part of the conversation was going, and wasn't sure he liked it.

"Well, Mr. Guest, you must realise that it is more urgent now than ever that we get in touch with your friend Finley. If, as we suspect might well be the case, that he is untouched by whatever is affecting the others who have come into contact with the prototype device, he might hold the secret to helping Miss Young and Mr. Potter. If you are incorrect, well then, it becomes even more urgent to find him before he exposes himself to any more danger."

"But we can't," Scott protested. "I can't.... I'll give you the data we've managed to collect from Bionamic so far. There's a memory card in my wallet. On it is all of the information you'll need. It's pushed up inside the lining of the flap on the coin-pouch."

"This one?" Woodroe asked, producing a small plastic square from an envelope.

"Right," Scott said, a bit chagrined that his

hiding place hadn't been as secure as he imagined. "I'll give you the password and I'll cooperate with you, but you can't bring in Finley, not yet."

"Why not?" Woodroe asked.

Scott paused, knowing that the only thing that might convince them would be the full story, something which might be difficult for closed government minds to accept.

"Okay then." He sighed. "If you thought this wasn't already, like so much bull, this'll doubtless be even harder for you to accept as true. You'll just have to be patient, can we get something to drink in here already, and hear me out, if that's even gonna be possible."

NINETEEN

I

Scott hoped he had convinced the FBI agents about the importance of Finley's mission. He had refused to divulge exactly where that mission would take him, only that Finley planned to visit an expert known to Professor Young who might be able to shed light on the situation. The feds were unimpressed by the story Finley had told Scott about what he'd seen in the resonance feedback. And despite all his talk of keeping an open mind, he couldn't really blame them. He had been hesitant to believe Finley too, at first.

Although he had withheld Professor Sabatini's name, Scott knew it would not take the feds long to identify all the possible acquaintances of Professor Young who were versed in the complexities of quantum physics. He had worried about this, but as the days passed by without word that Finley had been caught, he began to think that perhaps he had gotten through to the agents after all. By then, of course, he had other things to worry about.

He had kept the headaches to himself at first, partly because he wasn't sure if he was overreacting, but mostly because the idea of going to a hospital filled him with a dread he couldn't readily explain. His admission of having used the prototype device on a few occasions "just to try it out" however had resulted in an extensive, almost intrusive, medical check-up and the doctor's pointed questions showed that they already suspected that everything was not right.

With a bargaining technique he liked to think of as standing firm, but was characterised by the doctors as reckless stubbornness, he managed to avoid being sent to the hospital in exchange for agreeing to daily check-ups. The headaches weren't any worse than they had been before he was arrested, and he was not experiencing any of the other symptoms that

Sue had experienced, or Kim's colleague Potter. Still, the doctors mumbled to each other when they were doing their examinations, heads close together, occasionally glancing over at him, as if they were disappointed that he wasn't getting worse.

II

Finley sort of missed the freeway. Driving had been easy on the freeway; you knew that the road you were on led where you thought it would. At first he had reasoned that the anonymity of being among other cars would be his best bet, but after the second time he thought he heard a helicopter passing overhead, he had decided that the back roads would let him discover any pursuit more easily. Now he was glancing at his map again, wondering if the small dirt track branching off to the right was the road he had marked, or if it was a logging track that wouldn't be on the map at all. Before he could make up his mind, he had passed it and decided, partly because he didn't want to turn back, that it couldn't have been where he was supposed to turn.

Scott had called the previous day. Or more accurately someone using Scott's phone had tried to contact him. Finley had not picked up, deciding to upload any important information from the device onto his cloud service and then throw the thing out of the driver side window to be squashed by the next passing car. It wouldn't really be Scott calling, and if the FBI was using Scott's phone then the only use for Finley's phone was to paint a target on the roof of his car.

As Finley drove, he thought about what he was doing, why he was here. Scott and Sue had seemed to believe he was different somehow, that he was meant to be the one that could help Sue's uncle. Like it was his destiny or something. His mind briefly showed him a picture of himself in a cape, wearing a wizard's hat and he couldn't help but giggle briefly at the thought, but the reality of the situation soon reasserted itself. He didn't feel like any kind of wizard or superhero.

He had always imagined being The Chosen One—the one on which everyone's fate rested —would be an empowering feeling. That it would give him a driving sense of urgency, positive stress, an emphatic "Let's do this shit!"

Instead, he was growing more and more certain that he was going to get lost on the back roads to Phoenix and starve to death, leaving Professor Young and the others trapped forever. The only thing he felt was the pressure, and far from turning him into a diamond, it was threatening to reduce him to powder.

He shook his head, trying to disperse the dark foreboding clouds inside, concentrating on the next part of the drive. He had stopped at a gas station to get directions and make sure he was on track. The attendant had told him he could cut three hours off his drive if he found the right road down to the next town.

He turned at the next opportunity, almost certain that the road he had passed by had been the right one and that this one would turn out to lead to some local fishing hole or abandoned private property. Surprisingly, he soon found himself turning onto a large double lane thoroughfare that would lead him, if he could navigate the bewildering junction ahead, to the town centre.

It was a little bit like magic. A mere half hour earlier, Finley had been certain he was on the verge of being lost in the wilderness but now, in what seemed like moments, he was slowly moving through a vibrant area crowded with shoppers. He caught sight of a police car about to join the road some way ahead, so he pulled into a parking space and got out of the truck. As the police car cruised by slowly, clearly looking for something specific, Finley feigned interest in a toyshop window, where keeping track of the car's reflection as it passed by seemed far too easy.

He faltered briefly as a wave of dizziness hit him and he found himself leaning with one hand on the glass, his gaze focusing far beyond the toys inside, on a vision of his destination. He saw the house of Professor Sabatini, a lovely two-storey cabin set against a wooded area, and he also saw the black van parked a discreet distance away, as well as several other vehicles in a wider perimeter that he sensed rather than saw—vehicles the people in the black van would be able to call upon should they detect anything untoward.

"Excuse me, sir. Are you alright?"

The question made Finley pull himself together. He looked around to see the police car had stopped just past his own truck, and the officer inside was the one who had called out to him. Feeling a knot of dread form in his stomach, Finley walked towards the police car in what he hoped was a nonchalant way. He smiled and nodded.

"I'm fine. Just a bit dizzy. I haven't eaten all morning. Got so caught up in driving, I almost forgot," he told them, grabbing at the first lie he could think of. "I'll be fine once I get my blood sugar up."

"I hear ya," The officer said. "I'm the same way. I never go anywhere without a snack handy. You're not diabetic or something, are ya? Cause if it's an emergency I think I have an extra chocolate bar somewhere in here." The policeman's concern was a bit jarring compared to the disbelief Finley had been preparing for in his head, and it took him a moment to adjust. He waved off the offer.

"No, nothing like that, thanks all the same. I'll just go get myself something to eat and everything will be okay."

The policeman looked at Finley for a moment as if he was about to challenge him, then he just said. "Very well, sir. Just take care in future. We don't want you blacking out in traffic, now do we?"

"Point taken," Finley said, making a fist in his pocket, to have somewhere to focus his stress.

"Well, you have a nice day now, sir." The officer settled back into his seat. As the patrol car drove off, Finley turned and located the closest restaurant, making sure to head straight for it, in case he was being watched. Inside, he found that he hadn't been completely dishonest. He really was hungry.

* * *

Two hours later, Finley found himself in a beat-up motel room. He had paid for two nights under an assumed name, just to get access to a telephone that was not public and that could not be traced directly to him.

Knowing his vision to be true, but telling himself that it didn't have to be, he dialled the number for Professor Sabatini that he had somehow managed to obtain from the Professor's secretary at the university without very much trouble at all. The phone rang for what seemed to be far too long and when the connection was finally made, Finley half expected to have been redirected to voicemail. Instead a voice said hello in a manner that suggested that whomever it belonged to had been awoken by the telephone call.

"Is this Professor Sabatini?" Finley asked.

"I am Professor Sabatini, yes," the voice answered. "Who wants to know?"

"My name is Finley Demack, sir. I'm calling on behalf of Professor Young."

"Really? Professor Young from the UK, but he's never mentioned your name to me before." The tone of the voice suggested that the Professor was already suspicious of something.

"Yeah, we've only recently met. He's having one or two problems with his latest project into feedback research but due to unfortunate circumstances he's unable to contact you himself. I was hoping I might be able to visit you to discuss things."

There was a short pause, then the Professor cleared his throat. "That sounds acceptable. However, I'm not sure when I would be available. I'm under a lot of scrutiny at the moment, it isn't just clear to me when I'd get a chance to come away. If you tell me what kind of problems he is having, perhaps I can help you now."

Finley wasn't sure how much to read into the Professor's reply. Scrutiny could mean so many things. He wanted it to mean that the

Professor was aware that he was being watched, but Finely knew that the area of intersection in the Venn diagram of his life between things he *wanted* people to mean and what they *actually* meant had always been relatively small. He searched his brain for a way to inform the Professor without alerting anyone that might be listening in. "Well, the prototype he was building, for his current project, has had some unforeseen complications. Basically he is having a hard time disconnecting from the interface."

"The prototype will not disconnect?" The professor sounded confused.

"No," Finley said. "The actual prototype will disconnect easily enough, but the professor is having troubles."

There was a longer pause. "I think I understand. I think we do need to talk, but as I said I am a bit busy. I have an errand I need to run. Could you call back in an hour?"

Finley frowned. "I guess I could."

"Good, good. Just hang tight where you are and wait an hour before calling again and we'll have a proper conversation."

The line went dead and Finley looked at the silent receiver in his hand.

TWENTY

I

Hang tight?

Finley was lying on his hotel bed pondering Professor Sabatini's last words. Did he mean that he shouldn't leave the phone? He kicked off his shoes and reached for the remote for the tiny motel television, occasionally glancing at the phone. He was flipping lazily through the channels when the phone rang. He stabbed at the TV mute button and picked up the phone. It was the front desk telling him that there was an incoming call. Finley sat up higher on the bed, and asked them to put the call through.

"Mr. Demack?"

"Professor Sabatini!"

"Good! I was hoping you would catch my meaning. I need to warn you that I'm being watched and I think it might have something to do with Professor Young's work."

"Where are you now?"

"I'm in the bathroom, speaking on my daughter's cell phone. I don't think they're monitoring it, but we should get to the point quickly just in case they begin to suspect. Now tell me, what kind of trouble is Professor Young in?"

Finley took a deep breath swung his legs over the edge of the bed and started to talk. He was unsure if the professor was correct in his assumption, but he doubted that he would get a better opportunity than this. He told him everything, from gaining access to the quantum network, building their own prototype device and what he had experienced during his sessions with it. The professor listened patiently and without interrupting. Finley found himself checking several times that the other man was still on the line, each time he was told to go on.

When he had finished, Finley felt strangely drained. As if all his resolve had left him with the words. He had done it; he had delivered the message. His precious cargo of words had reached its destination. He could rest now?

"This is not good. Listen, Mr. Demack, I have been thinking of the ramifications of this ever since Young went missing, before, when he first told me about the resonance feedback. If my assumption is correct we have a very hazardous situation on our hands."

"Are Professor Young and the others in danger?"

"According to my calculations, we might all be in danger."

Finley briefly wondered if he had passed out on the bed and was dreaming this conversation. *Chosen one! You must save the world!* That kind of thing didn't happen. "What exactly is it you're describing here?"

"I believe that what has been dubbed the resonance feedback is in fact a pocket in space-time, a sort of buffer between this dimension and those nearby, for a given meaning of nearby of course, as normal spatial coordinates fail to make sense at that level. I fear that the current situation is interfering with the stability of the resonance."

"Which means...what? That it will break?"

"It might indeed be destroyed. The stuff of this dimension and the next might lose that which keeps them apart, and matter from different dimensions would attempt to co-exist in the same space."

"You mean this world and another would crash into each other?"

"In a manner of speaking, yes. I believe that if the contamination is not removed, several different universes might be colliding. The result would be disastrous beyond belief."

"And by contamination you mean?"

"Young and the others inside the resonance. They must be removed from there."

Finley licked his lips. He wasn't sure he understood whether what the professor was saying could even be possible, but it didn't really change his situation much—apart from infinitely raising the stakes, but that part was so much beyond belief that Finley found himself unable to worry about it. But possible or not, he still had to find out how to free those trapped in the resonance.

"What do I need to do?" he asked.

The professor sighed. "I must confess that I do not know. I have done several different calculations, based on different theories, but the only thing they show is that the access to this quasi-dimension must be shut down."

"Are you sure about this? I don't know much about physics but this sounds kind of strange to me."

"Everything about this is strange my friend. It shouldn't have worked to begin with. An antique box from Burma with secrets of quantum physics encoded on it? A virtual interface that allows you to mentally access a pocket dimension that isn't really part of the machine to begin with? I don't mind telling you that I'm out of my depth here, but if what Professor Young has told me is true, then I'm afraid it is very likely that we are all in severe danger."

"The box?" Finley asked. He hadn't thought of the Burmese box for some time and it was as if a nagging feeling in the back of his head had suddenly been identified. The box was clearly significant. He didn't yet know how, he just knew it was important.

"The Professor and his colleagues were working from information they gained from this artefact. A carved wooden box that contained hints that led to the breakthrough in quantum physics that allowed Young and Bionamic to develop their stable quantum connection."

Finley nodded to himself. "Yes. I know all about the box. I was just... Professor, is there any other information on this box?"

"There might be much information on it, or in it. We have yet to decode it in its entirety. Young believed there might be some sort of code in the decorative borders that—"

"No." Finley felt his vision blur out and he could almost see the box in front of him, spinning lazily in a black space. "I meant on the fourth side. There are three sides that relate to physics and then there is the fourth side. What's on that side?"

"How did you..." the Professor began, then seemed to think better of it. "I don't know that it relates."

"What is it though?" Finley could almost see the motif for himself now, the Professor's voice growing slightly muted in his ears as the vision started to take over.

"Well it's a bit of a mystery. Part of it is a representation of DNA with an encoded DNA sequence running along the edge of the symbol, continuing the scientific theme so to speak, but the rest seems to be religious gibberish about a saviour. I never paid it much attention as it isn't my area, it all sounds a bit contradictory."

Finley could see it clearly now, not close enough to read the text, but the symbol was there and in the background, holding the box, a shape forming. A human shape.

"Finley?" The Professor's voice broke through the vision, signalling Finley that he had probably been drifting off.

"Yes, Professor?"

"I said that the fourth side was probably not related, indeed it seems to contradict itself."

"Unless it's human DNA," Finley said, still clearing the sluggishness of the vision from his head. "Look, Professor. I'm gonna assume here that you have decided to trust me. If I give you an email address, can you send the information you have to it?"

"Are you sure they aren't monitoring your mail?"

"They probably are, but you aren't going to send it to me."

II

"There's something not right about all of this," Scott began. Kim tried to look attentive, but she was afraid he was about to set out on one of his speculative tangents again. She wasn't sure why they listened to him, she wasn't sure why he was allowed in the room, seeing as how he was currently under arrest. On the other hand, technically the only reason she wasn't under arrest was that Darius had vouched for her not running for it. As for Scott being there, she knew there had been extensive negotiations between him the FBI and Sytek, beginning at the moment the FBI noticed there was a notification on his mobile phone that he had a message waiting in "Atlantis". She remembered Atlantis was Scott's codename for the web-mail he used when he wanted to be anonymous.

The feds had managed to read the header of the message, and determine that it came from a Professor Sabatini, an old acquaintance of Professor Young, and that Finley's name as well as Professor Young's name figured in the subject line. She wasn't sure how the back-and-forths had worked out during those negotiations, but in the end Scott had agreed to let the FBI and Sytek get access to the message, provided that he was kept updated about what came of its contents.

When the message turned out to contain

information about Bionamic's research, the feds had turned to Sytek to make heads or tails of it. Darius, in turn had come to her to ask if Scott could be trusted or not. Somewhere in her answer, Darius had found a reason to make Scott part of the proceedings. She wished now that she knew exactly what it was.

It was kind of a relief, however, because it showed that both the FBI and Sytek were convinced enough about Bionamic being the "bad guys" that they'd rather conspire with the hackers than against them.

"They construct a device that implodes the quantum mind, connect it to God alone knows what, built from blueprints found in Burma, and they can't stop the people who are using it from getting sick!" Scott shouted. On the wall-screen, the contents of Finley's message were displayed, clear photographs of all sides of the Burmese box among them.

The federal agents glowered at him, but Kim could see there was a germ of a point in there somewhere.

"We think we know why," Igor said.

"We do?" Kim asked, surprised.

He shrugged. "Well, maybe. It's a theory at least. Like Finley suggests, the DNA code on this last side—this fourth side, as he calls it—is human DNA. What he's wrong about is assuming it's the fourth side. If we begin reading the sides of the box from the front." Igor started to rearrange the pictures of the different sides of the box. "And proceed around the box in turn in the same direction as the text is read, we get this order." Zooming in on the different tablets in turn, he continued. "The front is general physics information, encoded formulas and iconography that led Bionamic to their breakthroughs in quantum entanglement. On this side, the second tablet tells us about technical specifications needed for capturing the entanglement. Then, on the back is the DNA profile and the iconography mostly ignored by Bionamic talking about the chosen one. Then, and only then, do we get to the fourth side, which is the one indicating the possibility of somebody interfacing with the entanglement, leading to the creation of the prototype device that Potter and Professor Young have been using."

There was a short silence, then Ray spoke up. "So, basically what you're saying is that Bionamic got a free lunch from this thing? None of what they came up with was their idea to begin with?" He sounded disgusted.

Kim had been studying the line-up of images and thought she knew what Igor was getting at. "That's not quite what he's saying," she said. "He is saying that the tablets were meant to be read in this order and that Bionamic skipped a step. It's supposed to be: work out the theory, build the particle trap, find someone matching this DNA profile and then make the interface."

"Right," Igor confirmed.

"So the third tablet isn't actually talking about a saviour, just about the requirements to be able to use the interface safely?" Dave asked.

Igor nodded. "Which Bionamic ignored. They decoded the DNA and identified it as human, but when there didn't appear to be any immediate money to be made from it, they put that research on hold."

"It's Finley!" Scott exclaimed.

"What?" Kim said.

"Finley!" he repeated. "He has used the interface more than any of us without any symptoms. He's been the one seeing this other place while using it. Young and the others told him he was different. He must match the genetic profile."

"A perfect match?" Melanie scoffed. "What

are the odds of that?"

Scott shrugged. "I have no idea, but I bet none of you do either. How common is this particular set of genetic traits? It's not really a straightforward problem is it?"

Kim nodded. "Anyway, even if he isn't a perfect match, we can guess that he's closer than Sue or Potter, just by the fact that he hasn't been experiencing any of the symptoms they have."

O'Neill looked from face to face. "So what you are telling us is that Bionamic decided to experiment on people with a cutting edge technological device they built using instructions from a Burmese wood-carver and relying on scientific principles they barely understand to begin with?"

"Yep," Darius said, looking a little stunned at the prospect. "That seems to be the size of it."

"What morons," Woodroe concluded.

Kim couldn't disagree.

TWENTY-ONE

I

Finley's drive back had been an arduous one. He'd been driving the last 48 hours straight. There was an added sense of urgency now that he knew the world might be ending, a fact that still felt unreal. He had been distracted and preoccupied. Not by an impending apocalypse, however, but by Sytek. It was really his only choice if he wanted to get the information back to Professor Young, but he worried about the visions he kept having. They had been from different vantage points and different situations, but the common thread had been that Sytek was under surveillance by the forces that were trying to stop him.

Dawn broke, rousing him out of his introspection and he stopped at a gas station to buy some breakfast, which turned out to consist of a cup of strong coffee and an overpriced sandwich in a plastic container. Trying to meet with Sytek seemed even riskier in the sharp glare of the morning sun and he spent his morning formulating a plan in case things went sour.

After lunch, he chose an auto parts store off the main road and bought four canisters of puncture repair foam. After using it to prepare the Chevy's tyres so they were ready to handle an unforeseen event, or possible off-road escape should such a thing arise, Finley proceeded to scout out the meeting point.

The strip mall he had chosen was on the outskirts of town and closed early, so it would be more or less empty at the time he intended for the meeting. One side of the parking lot ended at a lightly wooded slope, at the bottom of which there was a bike path leading into town. It wasn't really suitable for cars, but with wheels filled with puncture repair foam, he was pretty sure the Chevy would survive both the slope and the dirt track; as for the stubborn cyclist he might encounter, *well*, Finley thought, *One thing at once.*

Making a mental note of the best place to wait on the car park, he made the call to Sytek.

II

"I think we should have called the number Woodroe gave us," Igor said as Darius guided his corvette towards the meeting spot that Finley, the final hacker, had chosen.

"You heard the guy," Darius replied. "He will be ready to run at the slightest provocation. The fact that he's still on the run shows that he's good at avoiding the feds. In this case, I think they would be more of a hindrance than a help. Also I would actually like to talk to him before O'Neill and Woodroe get their hands on him."

"What about Max and his freelance fake agents?" Igor carried on sounding as though the nerves were starting to build. "I know we haven't heard from him lately, but I don't think he's been sitting on his hands. I imagine he is pretty ticked off right now that we haven't sided with him."

"The only reason Max was getting riled up is

because he knows he's finally losing some of his control. He's backed himself into a corner, that's all."

"That's all? You know what they say about cornered animals."

"Look, I know you aren't suggesting we call up Max and tell him everything, so if you've got a better idea about how we might get further information about this virtual connection, what it is and what it's done to Potter, then I'd like to hear it."

Igor stayed silent and Darius sighed.

"At least we aren't breaking any laws. Maybe a few rules of propriety, but no laws. We'll meet with the guy, hopefully convince him to come in peacefully, and if we can't, the FBI wonder boys won't be worse off than they were before. I'm sure it will be fine."

"I hope I don't have to remind you of that statement."

"You know sometimes you've just got to say 'what the hell' and go for it. We've already burned most of our boats with Max so there's no use trying to save the project. None of us are gonna starve. We'll just go back to where we were before his proposal. Plus a lawsuit, perhaps. But I reckon the thought of a countersuit concerning the safety of my employees will keep him from doing that.

"And I'm pretty sure the FBI will understand too. And even if they don't, they can't really arrest us. We'll bounce back. You'll see."

"This'll be after we've filed for bankruptcy, then?" Igor joked, finally relinquishing the gloom. "I can understand why we're doing this, I'm just having a hard time believing it. Despite your assurances, I don't think Max will take this lying down. Somehow he'll find a way of enforcing the small print. This has to be in breach of our contract."

"Stuff him!" Darius growled. "I don't like the man he's shown himself to be. I should have listened to Kim from the start. As for his contract, well I have a pretty good idea what he can do with it. If there is a chance of saving Potter and a chance of pissing off Max, quite honestly I'll try for both." After a brief pause, he added, "Come on, Igor. You do want to meet the promised saviour, don't you?"

With the sunlight fading beneath leaden skies, they noticed the brightly lit glass foyer of a cinema from the road. Turning into the mall parking lot, Darius kept left, as per instruction, and stopped. The single pickup truck near the far end of the car park flashed its lights once.

"That must be him." Darius said, and set their car in motion towards the truck.

Igor's phone began to ring. He declined the call and shortly after there was a text message. "It's from Melanie," he informed Darius. "Seems Max has called the lab several times during the last thirty minutes, demanding to speak with us."

"Looks like he really is checking up on us after all."

"Yeah. I just hope he isn't paying too close attention to all of this."

Drawing up alongside the truck, Darius noticed the driver had turned off the cab lighting, hiding his features in darkness. It wasn't until the man opened his window and leaned out and looked down at the Corvette did his features become clear. He looked scruffy, which was expected since he'd been on the road for so long, but his gaze was attentive. "You must be Finley?"

"And you're Darius?"

"That's right."

"You're on your own? As in nobody followed you?"

"Nobody followed us in here. I can't say for

sure about the road here."

Finley replied in a nod, as if the answer had met with his approval.

"I'd ask for some sort of promise of safety here, but I doubt that's an option. If I am to come in, however, I do need some assurances. Also, I'll need to use your prototype interface."

Darius shook his head slowly. "I'm not sure that'll be possible. Even if I assured you that it was, it wouldn't count for much. We're in the middle of an FBI investigation and the lab is being watched day and night. I have no sway over the FBI and any attempt to smuggle you in or any of our technology out would be very risky. I could tell you differently," he added. "But then I'd be lying."

Finley looked even more nervous, glancing around the parking lot as if he expected the feds to show up at any moment. It made Darius nervous too and he caught himself surveying his surroundings.

"I want you to know that I didn't call them in. That was a decision made by Bionamic. We are just cooperating with the FBI as we are legally bound to do."

Staring at Darius, clearly trying to work out if he could trust him, Finley nodded slowly.

Darius decided it was time to try to push. "I can't promise you it will happen, but I can promise you that if you play fair with us, Sytek will not press charges against you and I will put in a word on your behalf with the agents investigating the case."

"I know words are cheap," Igor said, "but you can trust Darius. If he says he's going to help, he will."

Darius was about to affirm that Igor spoke the truth when the sound of cars intensified interrupting his thoughts.

Finley was pondering the words of Darius and his friend when the sounds of the cars reached them. He didn't think Darius had sold him out. As far as he could tell, the man was on the level. Also if he had been laying a trap, he would have waited until he got more information before springing it.

Finley cranked the Chevy into gear and was about to floor the accelerator when his current surroundings faded out. Before him, he saw cars entering the parking lot and proceeding to block all the exits as well as vehicles equally matched with his own ready to follow him along his planned bike path escape route. Hitting the steering wheel, Finley opened the door and jumped out between the two cars, trying to decide if he should take his chances on foot.

A large black GMC Yukon had pulled up behind the truck. Another had screeched to a halt in front, boxing both his and Darius's vehicle in. Finally, a gold coloured classic Lincoln town car rolled to a stop on the other side of Darius's vehicle.

Darius and his companion were also getting out of their car to confront the two men in dark suits that exited the Lincoln. One of them, a shorter, stocky man with a grim expression, wandered over to them.

"Hello, Darius," he said. "You and Igor can forget that you were ever here and go away now. We're bringing your friend in to have a little chat about what's been going on."

The man was young, somewhere in his twenties, carrying a presence way beyond his years. Finley noted that Darius shrank back slightly from him.

"Come on, Darius. You don't know me, but I can assure you that when I'm hired to do a job, I do it. We're bringing him in and you can't stop us. Why not just leave and save yourself a whole lot of trouble." The car blocking their exit tiptoed forward until it was only blocking Finley's truck. Finley suppressed the instinct to tell Darius not to leave him, knowing there was no way he would be any safer if they stayed. And if they did, it might only get them hurt in the process. Finley saw Darius look back at him and then his resolve hardening. Before either could make another move, however, the parking lot was flooded with lights as several more cars, lights flashing on their roofs, entered and surrounded them.

"This is the FBI," said a voice over a bullhorn. "Everybody stay where you are."

One of the Yukons started to drive away, but when a shot rang out they stopped. Climbing out of a black Mercedes were two men that Finley vaguely recognised. He assumed they must be the FBI officers he had seen through the web-cam hidden outside Sue's house. The taller man gestured towards where Finley, Darius and Igor were standing and the pair started walking towards them as police officers piled out of cars all around, ordering people out of cars and distributing handcuffs like they were mardi gras necklaces.

When they were within talking distance, Darius held up his hands. "Before you say anything, agent O'Neill, I know we should have called you. I just didn't want to tear you away from your work."

"This *is* our work," the man identified as O'Neill said, and his colleague nodded in agreement. "I won't hold it against you though. I'm just happy I had this chance to bring in Max's impostor agents." He turned to the imposing man, who was less imposing at the moment as he was face down over the hood of his car, being handcuffed. "Impersonating federal agents is, unsurprisingly, a federal offense. You are now in a lot of trouble."

Finley watched this new situation unfold. As far as he could tell he was in much the same difficulty, only slightly improved by the fact that these were the proper authorities and slightly less likely to hurt him.

"And you must be Finley Demack. We've been searching all over for you. I look forward to talking to you."

Finley tried to think quickly. If they arrested him and brought him in it could be days before he could convince them to even let him talk to Sytek, not to mention actually setting foot there. "I'm ready to tell you everything you want to know. If you let me do it at the Sytek offices," he said.

"What is it with all these demands these days?" O'Neill asked.

"Nuisance," replied his colleague.

"And I take it that if we don't take you there you are going to be difficult?"

Finley nodded. "I'm afraid so. What I've got to tell is very important and it's best told at Sytek."

O'Neill sighed, then smiled. "Very well. Any other requests?"

"I want Sue and Scott there too. They can corroborate parts of my story."

"The presence of Scott Guest is something we can arrange. Your friend Sue, on the other hand, is still unconscious and in the hospital."

Finley felt his stomach clench in worry. "She's in a coma? Like the others?"

"That's right," Darius cut in. "What do you know about that, Finley? Anything that could help?"

"At Sytek," he said. "I'll tell you everything I know at Sytek."

TWENTY-TWO

I

Kim had been both happy and sad to see Finley brought in. Happy because he was alright, but disappointed that his flight from justice had been cut short. She knew he wouldn't have been able to keep on the run forever, but it still felt strangely like defeat. She was also a bit confused about why he had been brought into Sytek.

A quick meeting had been called and Finley had told his story to all those present. Kim hadn't heard the entire story of what had happened after the others had taken to the road and was interested from the beginning. She didn't know what to think about his stories about having visions, but Scott stood by Finley's assurances that it was the truth. Finley's tale of interfacing with the resonance feedback, however, sucked her into the story completely and the revelation of what Professor Sabatini had told him was a hammer blow at the end. Hard to believe—almost impossible, in fact—but there was no doubt that Finley was telling the truth about what he had been told, and it seemed to Kim that on some level he believed it. If Professor Sabatini was being truthful or, for that matter, correct, was something she could only guess at. When Finley stopped talking the room was quiet.

"Did Max know about this possibility and go ahead anyway, I wonder?" Darius said.

"It does sound pretty incredible," Ray said. "I can understand a sceptical approach. Still, once your people start getting sick while using your device, going ahead unchecked does seem either stupid or callous."

"I guess they thought they were minimizing their risks when they decided to just use it for the quantum internet," Finley said. "It's not like the public would have the know-how to put together an interface device like the one Bionamic created. I mean, we managed it, but probably not perfectly and only because we had access to the plans."

"So they tried to stop you because you had that knowledge?" Melanie asked.

"I doubt it," Finley mused. "I'm thinking it's just standard corporate greed. They bought that artefact for a lot of money. They probably feel that the knowledge gleaned from it belongs to them."

"Also they aren't gonna be happy if people found out about them putting their own workers into a coma," Scott added.

"That too," Finley agreed.

O'Neill looked sceptical. "So why here?" he asked. "You said it was important that you tell your story here. Regardless of whether I believe your story or not, I don't really see the need. We could have given your statement to Sytek after debriefing you elsewhere."

"The interface device is here. I need to use it to talk to Professor Young again. I have to let him know what Professor Sabatini told me."

"Not a chance. One of Darius's men could do that."

"It would take way too long for them to acclimatise themselves. Also, I'm the only one who has managed to free myself from the resonance after being fully acclimatised to it."

"So, we're back to you being the saviour then?" O'Neill asked.

"Huh?" Finley didn't seem to understand and Kim felt the need to step in.

"The DNA on the box, Fin. We think it's there to describe the sort of person who can interface with the entanglement without being negatively affected. Since you are the only one who's experienced no problems, we figured..."

"That it described me?" Finley said. "Or someone like me."

"Exactly," Kim said. "I think we should let him do it." She took the opportunity to address the room while she had everyone's attention.

Scott nodded enthusiastically. "We have to, given the stakes."

"Supposed stakes," Darius chimed in, then he shrugged. "But I don't see what harm it will do. If Finley is sure he will not be affected by the interface, it doesn't really matter all that much if he's wrong about the rest, does it? If he's right, however..."

Everybody looked at O'Neill and Woodroe. The two agents looked at each other, then O'Neill looked at Finley and spoke. "I'm having a hard time believing most of the things you've just told us here today," he said, then he reached out and turned off the voice recorder that he had been capturing Finley's statement with. "But it's not like you can run off if we strap you to a chair. Just let us get this statement typed up in triplicate and have you sign them, then you can have an hour to do whatever experiments you want."

II

As if wakened from a dream, Finley had once again slipped from reality. He was back again and it felt more familiar than it had any right to be. Still, something was different this time. He wasn't just observing; he was there in a way he hadn't felt before, bristling with the sort of awareness reserved for seers and prophets.

Somehow he knew where he would find Professor Young and moved in that direction, passing through glowing green walls, walking along surfaces at many angles. On the way, he passed the room where the half-formed visitor had been to find that the humanoid shape had taken the features of a man. Finley guessed that this must be Potter. Another body was forming in the next room. A woman. *Sue.* He paused to lay a reassuring hand on her shoulder, uncertain whether she was aware of him.

He found Professor Young, Mathew and Patrick in the room where he had first appeared. At least it looked exactly like the one where he had appeared, but he wasn't sure. They all looked up as he entered, Mathew with a smile, Patrick with what looked like practiced indifference and Professor Young with something that resembled hope lighting his eyes. The Professor got up and came to greet him.

"Welcome back, Finley! I hope you bring us good news."

Finley grimaced and acknowledged the other with dignity. "I'm afraid not, but I do bring news. Perhaps it will help you."

Finley quickly related what had happened since the last time he was there and then told them about as much of Professor Sabatini's materials as he had managed to memorise in the time he had been allowed by the two FBI agents. Professor Young listened carefully, occasionally asking him to repeat something he had said, then repeating it back to him to make sure he had it correctly. When he was finished, there was another of those silences. None of his audience was sceptical of his claims this time, though. This silence was maintained out of a desire not to disturb Professor Young's thoughts.

Mathew and Finley watched the old man move his lips silently with closed eyes, while Patrick wandered about the room, occasionally changing the surface he walked on. After what felt like an age, Professor Young opened his eyes again. "Yes. He could be right. And his research definitely talked about there being a centre to this pocket dimension? A place where it touches all the dimensions it is separating at once?"

Finley nodded. "Yes. He thought that this room you cannot enter might be this place."

"Then I think that's where we must go. If it touches all the dimensions in that place, then that must be the easiest place to reach our own dimension. Maybe we can get back through there."

"But we've tried already." Patrick said from the ceiling where he was lying, "Forgotten already Melvin? We tried lots and lots of times to no avail."

"I know, Patrick, but what's the harm in trying again? Perhaps Finley can help us do what we could not?"

Patrick shrugged and did a handstand on his surface, suddenly dropping down to join the rest of them. "Maybe. Maybe not," he said. "I do like the word avail, though."

Professor Young smiled at him kindly. "Tell you what. If it doesn't work, you can use it again." Patrick nodded.

"And even if it does," Finley added. "I'm sure we will find some use for it just the same."

This being settled, the four of them set off towards the solid room. Standing before it, Finley could not discern it from any other space in the world they were in. It had the same semi-translucent walls, and seemed to be completely empty, but when Mathew walked up to it and pressed his weight against it, he couldn't move through.

When Mathew was done, Patrick had to have a go. He tried to sneak up on it by walking up the surface of the wall and then jumping up and down while looking very concentrated. When he had given up, Finley looked at Professor Young who indicated that Finley should try.

Taking a breath—which he wasn't sure if he needed in this place, but which felt like the real thing—he took a step forward and walked straight through the wall. Once inside, he looked back at his recent friends, their anxious faces and searching stares telling him that they could no longer see him.

He turned around again and examined the space he was in. It was not an ordinary place, not even in the extraordinary world he was now in. There was a feeling of sanctity, and a sense of timelessness pervading the pyramid-shaped room. In the middle was what looked like a table or a plinth of some sort with a large multifaceted crystal on top.

Looking closer, Finley saw movement inside. Apprehensive at first, he soon moved closer, to find the movement were dozens of Finleys moving towards him, and the central plinth, as he neared the crystal. There was something strange about these other Finleys and he drew even closer to examine them.

When he had reached the crystal he could tell what had caught his eye. No two of the reflections were exactly alike, and none of them was an accurate reflection of him. He waved his hand uncertainly in front of the crystal and all the little reflections of him did the same, but none in exactly the same way.

Then he could feel them. Their presences, their thoughts, bleeding into his own and he moved even closer, so close that his breath, if he had any, should have fogged up the surface of the crystal. Slowly, reverently he reached out to touch the top of the crystal, the hands of the others reaching out with him, now in perfect synchronicity.

Unsure of what to expect, and still feeling the smooth shiny surface beneath his palm, Finley was surprised when the crystal began to melt, forming a tight seal around his hand. With only his wrist remaining visible, the uncompromising grip triggered the onset of an inner wakefulness, against which any attempt to resist would surely be to no avail. *See Patrick? I got it in there anyway.*

He began to feel himself stretched out into what seemed to be infinity, the borders between where he ended and the next version of him started impossible to discern, eventually stretching them all out into one continuous band of light. The pulsating waves of energy that passed through him should have been uncomfortable, painful even, but the only thing

Finley felt was the certainty that together they would be able to fix all of it.

EPILOGUE

Burma – 1063 B-C-E

Finley Demack sat at a wooden bench in his small dwelling looking at the piece of wood in front of him. He liked it here. He liked his work. If anyone had told him before he came here that he would be happy living a life without an internet connection where he made a living using his hands, he would have laughed at them, but that was in another life, one he only half remembered. He smiled and ate a piece of fruit before returning to his work. He had ordered the wood specially and had laid out his tools with extra care this morning. This was the day he began.

He closed his eyes and recalled to his inner sight the one memory of his old life that had not dimmed with time. That which was indelibly imprinted in his mind.

The wooden box appeared against a background of black space, resting in the hands of a human figure. This time he knew who the figure was without having to look. The man who held the box up for his inspection was Finley Demack. All of them, from everywhere, and he was smiling.

Finley opened his eyes, picked up a chisel and set about his work.